CARLY REID

Mince Pies and Murder

First published by Inkpot Books 2019

First edition

This book was professionally typeset on Reedsy.
Find out more at reedsy.com

Contents

Yule Night

Jessica Greer paused for a moment before she entered *Lissa's,* the charming coffee shop that belonged to her friend Ealisaid Robertson. Not normally open in the evening, Ealisaid had made an exception for Dalkinchie's annual Yule Night. There had been a hum of anticipation around the village for weeks, and Jessica was delighted to be reporting on the event for her job as a junior reporter for *The Drummond and Dalkinchie Herald.* It would help to take her mind off the intrusive memories she had been having lately.

The cafe – Ealisaid's pride and joy – was a cheerful, homey spot all year round, but looked especially so tonight in contrast to the dark, frosty night outside. Ealisaid had placed a small tree in the corner, and wound delicate strands of multicolored lights around the shelves behind the counter. She had added Christmassy flavors to her drinks menu, with spiced coffee syrups and flavored teas. Tonight, she wasn't serving food apart from Christmas cake. This took pride of place on the polished counter at the front – with a whole, beautifully iced and decorated cake raised up on one of Ealisaid's stands, and small slices temptingly arranged next to it, allowing customers to help themselves.

"Hello, you! Glad you made it before I ran oot," said Ealisaid, gesturing. "The cake has been popular already. Help yourself!"

Jessica didn't need to be asked twice. She took a moment to admire the beauty of the sugar craft on display, and was soon fully appreciating the warm, sweet flavors of her sample slice. She had already tried one from the same batch, and knew that her aunt Reenie had ordered another one from Ealisaid for their own Christmas. Ealisaid took only a limited number of orders, and as she finished off her small slice, Jessica felt all the more fortunate to be looking forward to more of the same.

Ealisaid was selling teas and coffees from her usual spot behind the counter, and had set up a makeshift extra counter by arranging a couple of tables together perpendicular to it, in front of the long back wall. Behind this, seated between two crockpots and working on something behind the table, sat Murdo Smith, Ealisaid's part-time assistant. The son of a local dairy farmer, Murdo was a friendly soul, and he greeted Jessica warmly when he noticed her.

"Lovely to see you Jessica, Merry Christmas! Can I get you a hot chocolate? Wi', or wi'out a wee added special something?" He gestured at the crockpots. Somebody – probably either Ealisaid or her younger sister Mairead, who often worked in the café, too – had written signs to sit beside each one, indicating the presence or absence of a dash of whisky. Jessica elected for the alcohol-free option – after all, she was technically working, even if she didn't think her editor Grant Mack would mind. Murdo began to serve the drink, and as he did so, laid down a bundle of knitting.

"What's that you are working on, Murdo?"

Jessica had seen some of the items Murdo had knitted before, in particular a hat for his brother Magnus, who sometimes worked alongside Jessica as a photographer for *The Herald.* She knew that Murdo had been very strongly influenced by the woman he called 'his wee granny', and that she had been the one who had taught him how to knit.

Murdo handed Jessica her drink and she wrapped her cold hands around it gratefully. He held up his knitting needles and displayed the beginnings of his project – navy blue, with a Fair Isle pattern.

"It'll be a wee cardigan for one o' DI Gordon's twins. I've already done the other one. It wis a wee bitty complicated, but I'm fair chuffed wi' how it's turned oot. It's their first Christmas, see, and I just wanted to give them something a bit special. I know the Detective Inspector is looking forward to a big family Christmas wi' his partner and the babies, I think there's other folk going to be traveling over and it's the first time they'll have met the twins. Loads o' photies, probably."

In addition to his duties on the family farm and his job at *Lissa's,* Murdo also volunteered as a Special Constable in the police force, making DI James Gordon his boss. Jessica, charmed with the notion, exclaimed in delight.

"Oh, they will look so sweet! I've got twin sisters you know, and they were so cute wearing matching clothes when they were small. He'll be really pleased, Murdo! What a kind gift."

Murdo looked abashed. "Aye, well, 'tis the season..."

But before he could continue, an altercation broke out at the front of the shop. A man, turning to leave after being served his takeaway drink by Ealisaid, had clearly walked straight into a small child's flashing wand – and was not taking it well.

"Watch oot!" The man stopped and looked round where he stood, his face twisted in disgust. He wore a heavy dark grey woolen coat over battered blue jeans, paired with scuffed hobnail boots. A worn-through patch on the arm of his coat had been mended, badly, using a clashing thread. His shoulders curved forwards, and a shock of graying hair stood up over his thick, beetling brows.

The child, a tiny girl of about six, had turned pink and looked as if she was on the verge of tears. She lowered her wand slowly. Her father then leaned forward and intervened, gently ushering his daughter behind him as he spoke.

"Aye, OK, Ian – no harm done. She's just excited, all the weans are. It's a special night."

"Well, she shouldnae be waving that thing around. You need to keep a better eye on her. And those wands are just trash anyway. It'll be broken in no time. Waste of money if you ask me."

Before anyone could respond to that, the surly man sloped out of the café and turned right, heading up the hill towards The Ram's Heid Inn, Dalkinchie's local pub. Ealisaid successfully broke the shocked silence left behind by offering the child a striped peppermint candy cane, and smiling warmly at her family before returning to the counter to finish preparing their drinks.

Jessica turned back to Murdo.

"Ian Johnston," he said with a nod in the direction of the door. "No' the most pleasant of men usually, but you'd think at Christmas he'd find it in his heart to have a wee bit o' cheer. Imagine upsetting a wean like that. Ach well. Some people."

"Is he a local, then?" Jessica asked.

"Have ye no' come across the Johnstons before? Two brothers, both electricians. And both – I'll say it, although I shouldnae – as grumpy as each other. Although while Ian Johnston is away up to the pub, by the looks of it, his brother is daein' something quite different..."

Murdo leaned in closer to continue, mindful that there were still children in the café and not wanting to be overheard. "…he's Santa. On the float? Bill Johnston does Santa's grotto every year on Yule Night. You'll see him later, although you won't recognize him. He's actually awfy good at being Santa, although he's a real bah humbug aw' the rest of the year."

A pair of grumpy brothers. If what Murdo had said was true, how, Jessica wondered, could someone capable of being so unpleasant and surly have taken up the role of waving and smiling at the children from the float, in a Santa suit? Perhaps, she reasoned to herself, Bill Johnston was a little more pleasant than his brother – even if only a little. She glanced back towards the little girl with the sparkly wand again. For the sake of the children, she certainly hoped so.

* * *

The street crowd had thinned by the time Jessica left, probably because they were all already waiting for the official beginning of the evening – and Santa's departure – at the courtyard outside The Ram's Heid. Jessica decided to hurry up there too, but paused to look across the High Street towards The Bloom Room. The little flower shop – her Aunt Reenie's fledgling business – looked beautiful, its painted sign reflecting a warm glow from the windows beneath, in which there were colorful floral displays, reds and greens predominating. Jessica knew that Reenie would be giving out sparkling wine or orange and cranberry juice, and hoping to get a few more Christmas orders before the holidays truly began.

Walking over and peeking into the shop, she saw that the upturned wooden crates used as shelving – some with Christmas wreaths or floral decorations and others with the balms and sprays that Reenie had begun selling – were now decorated with star-shaped white fairy lights. A Christmas display with a tree-shaped decoration of holly and lights stood right in the centre of the shop floor. Feeling a glow of pride for how the shop had developed after its rocky start, Jessica waved at Reenie through the window, and Reenie, glancing up, waved back briefly, busy dealing with a customer.

The frosty night couldn't be more perfect. People, already muffled up in thick coats and cozy scarves, stamped their feet and wrapped their arms around themselves to get warmer. Children, many up past their usual bedtime and bundled into heavy brightly-colored coats, sang snatches of Christmas carols that they had learned at daycare and school. Some waved more of the light-up plastic wands which an enterprising person dressed as Santa Claus was selling further down the High Street.

Jessica, keen to take in as much as she could of the mood as well as the sights, began to jot down her impressions in her notebook. The Dalkinchie Yule Night event happened every year in December, always on the third Friday, but this was Jessica's first experience of it. She had lived in Dalkinchie for six months now, since joining her Aunt Reenie earlier in the year to help set up the flower shop. Her part-time role for the local newspaper had been an excellent way to get to know the village and its inhabitants – even if it had occasionally thrown her in the path of more extreme circumstances as well.

Jessica flexed her fingers. She was wearing fingerless gloves so that she could still use a pen, but the cold was creeping in, numbing her hands and making writing increasingly difficult. She closed her notebook, and hooked her pen into its elastic closure.

A crowd had gathered on the paved area outside The Ram´s Heid. It was a charming old black-and-white coaching inn, formed of a long, asymmetric stone building. It was largely painted white but the surrounds of its tall multi-paned windows were black, giving it a striking, almost medieval appearance. The entrance way was large and arched, and right outside it – unusually – stood a low wooden platform stage with a podium in its centre. It was flanked on either side by a burning log, which hissed and crackled in the cold air. Christmas lights ran all along the front of the building, and stretched over the top of the stage to the other side of the street – though none of them were yet lit up.

This was where the evening kicked off every year, with the switching-on ceremony followed by a procession of a horse-drawn float through the High Street, transporting Santa Claus along with a couple of his elves to the Village Hall at the other end of the village, whereupon children could visit Santa in his grotto. Some residents of the village would always follow behind the float, eager to be first in the queue for the grotto – and for the tea and mince pies that were served up there. Other villagers would take advantage of the fact that every shop in Dalkinchie was participating by staying open late, offering special discounts on products and services, and usually serving refreshments of their own.

Just as the crowd's mood seemed about to turn from excitement to impatience, there was some movement at the stage in front of the pub. The MacNaughton, Dalkinchie's local celebrity and clan chief, was due to initiate the proceedings, and he had come out of the pub with a young woman. The great bearded Scotsman was wearing his kilt as usual, along with a thick sweater, scarf and dark blue woolly hat pulled over his thick head of hair. The young woman was in overalls, hair tied back out of her face in a single plait that fell over one shoulder. The pair climbed onto the platform, the woman gesturing and speaking to Gillespie MacNaughton who did not yet address the crowd, instead nodding and replying to her quietly. Jessica watched as he appeared to ask a question, and, apparently unable to answer, the woman climbed back down off the platform and disappeared back into the pub. The MacNaughton beamed at the waiting crowd and bellowed:

"No' long now, folks! Just a wee technical hitch!"

There were minor grumblings, but for the most part the crowd seemed content to wait. The foot stamping and jumping increased. A child's small, clear voice rang above the crowd "I want to see Santa!" Jessica overheard someone next to her murmur "I wonder where he's got tae – Santa's usually here by noo."

The young woman reappeared, this time accompanied by another man, this one much shorter and thinner than the MacNaughton. The pair moved behind the platform together and briefly fiddled with the cables there, before the man traced the length of cable to behind the podium and pushed something there. Job seemingly done, he stepped down from the platform and went back towards the pub. All eyes then turned back to the MacNaughton, who began to address the crowd.

All eyes, that is, apart from Jessica's. She was still watching the thin man as he spoke abruptly to the young woman outside the pub, and stomped off back inside without a backwards glance towards her or the crowd. Jessica wasn't close enough to hear what he had said, but the young woman's reaction was clear enough. Bathed in the light from the pub window, her face had turned red. Her eyes were glittering, her lips pressed together.

After a moment, she caught Jessica looking at her. Swiftly she broke eye contact, looked down and turned away. Head still bowed, she moved over closer to the podium, and then walked behind the platform.

"Merry Christmas, Dalkinchie!"

Perhaps mindful of the delay and the cold, the MacNaughton had kept his speech very short. He now deftly flicked the switch below the podium and the village was suddenly illuminated by hundreds of Christmas lights. Being from the U.S., Jessica was no stranger to holiday light displays, and in fact the village efforts had seemed a little low-key from her perspective when she had seen them being constructed. Now, however, the warm white lights gave the whole village a magical feel. From the Inn itself at the top of the street, the lights ran along to and wrapped around the great nearby Christmas tree, as well as lighting up the many smaller trees which were attached to each building frontage all along the High Street. In addition, there was a pretty canopy of lights slung between the buildings, from one side of the street to the other. Jessica immediately thought of The Bloom Room – it was already looking charmingly Christmassy, and she couldn't wait to see what it looked like now, with the outside lighting as well.

The horses attached to the float had been waiting patiently during the delay and the lighting up ceremony, with only the occasional harrumphs or whinnies. The elves, however, were clearly feeling the cold through their thin outfits and had been looking quite miserable – not that Mairead Robertson ever really looked cheerful exactly. Now, Santa Claus himself emerged from the pub in all his red-suited glory, and with a couple of muffled cries of "Ho, ho, ho!", he hastily swung himself into the chair on the float, lounged back comfortably with one hand across his belly, and began waving at the children.

The float slowly moved off, with the clicking of the horses' hooves easily heard over the hubbub of voices. Soon the crowd fell in behind the float, and started to move along behind it. Jessica hung back slightly. As she started to walk slowly down the High Street, she took one last look back at the scene outside the Ram's Heid. The MacNaughton had now climbed off the platform and was talking to an elderly man outside the pub. There was no sign of the young woman.

* * *

The procession moved slowly behind the cart all the way to the Village Hall. Jessica looked into the windows of all the shops as she passed by, enjoying the view of Dalkinchie at Christmas now that the lights had been switched on. Gillespies, the fine dining restaurant near the Hall, had outdone themselves with two columns of lights wrapped round the door jambs and a tableau of golden reindeer to one side of their tiled entryway. Jessica saw a party of women sitting at the table in the window. One of them, a woman with long shiny blonde hair, blew into a party whistle as Jessica went past.

Santa's Grotto had taken over one of the smaller rooms at the front of the Village Hall building, and Jessica edged past the waiting line to make her way through to the larger main hall at the back. There, teas and coffees and other refreshments were being sold, and a local community choir was performing a variety of Christmas music on stage. Around the edges of the hall, various stalls had been set up. The primary school fundraising committee was selling hot chocolate, gingerbread reindeer – each one individually decorated with swirls and splodges of multicolored icing – and bath bombs with enthusiastic dollops of glitter on the top of each one. There was a bottle tombola stall, at which people were already paying for the chance to win a fine bottle of Scotch whisky, although the only prize that had been secured so far was a small bottle of shampoo.

Right at the back corner was the stall where Jessica now headed, currently manned by her editor Grant Mack. It was selling diaries and calendars, published by the press collective that also ran *The Herald*, and Jessica had promised to take a shift in order to let Grant spend some time taking in the Yule Night event as well. Her boss lived with and cared for his mother, but as Jessica could see Mrs Mack safely ensconced at one of the tea tables with a crowd of women from The Guild, she had a sneaking suspicion where Grant might go first. Since the summer, he and her Aunt Reenie had grown steadily closer. Reenie downplayed their relationship, telling Jessica that it was a friendship and nothing more, and that both of them were too busy for anything else. It didn't stop Jessica thinking there was more to it, and she was sure Grant would make a beeline for The Bloom Room straight after leaving the Hall.

Jessica greeted Grant warmly. He had been a huge support to her, first offering the job that had enabled her to stay in Dalkinchie, then supporting and mentoring her as a journalist. "Hey, how are things going so far?"

"Sales have been steady! I think we will have more yet, though, many people went straight for the tea and mince pies. The calendars are especially popular. They make such a good gift, easy to post, and the photography this year is quite lovely."

Jessica agreed. The calendar featured local landscape scenes and it showcased the beauty of this lush, green part of Scotland perfectly. *The Herald* ran the competition to select the twelve images. Magnus Smith had been a judge. This meant that he himself did not have any photos in the calendar, which Jessica thought was a shame as his own work was every bit as good.

"Right, I'll be off then Jessica, if that's OK with you?" Grant continued. "I'll be back later to pack up here at the stall, and to pick up my mother and escort her home. The calendar is five pounds, remember, and the diary is ten – I've learned from experience to try and minimize the amount of change I need to have, although there is some there in the cash box if you need it."

"I'm sure I won't have any problems, Grant," Jessica replied. "I'll get selling! Enjoy your evening, and I'll see you later."

"Thanks Jessica. I'm going to nip down and see your aunt first – I've been meaning to order a small centerpiece for Christmas dinner."

Jessica smiled to herself. Did Grant really think she was that stupid? He didn't need an excuse to go and visit Reenie. A centerpiece, indeed.

Sales continued to be steady over the next twenty minutes or so. The diaries were beautifully produced with week-to-view across two pages, a ribbon marker and quality hard covers. Jessica thought she might buy one herself if there were any left at the end of the evening. Although as she browsed through the months of the following year, her internal voice began to nag at her. She had deferred her place at journalism graduate school back home in order to spend one year in Scotland, and the months in Dalkinchie were flying past faster than she would like. Soon it would be decision time again.

Perhaps because it was Christmas, the events of a year before had been playing on her mind, the Christmas she had spent with her ex-boyfriend Mike and his family. It had been the first time she had ever spent Christmas Day away from her mom and dad, sisters and brother, and at the time it had signaled the seriousness of her relationship with Mike. They had all discussed the plans the two were making to live together and attend grad school in the same city. One year later felt like a lifetime. What would the next year bring? Where would she be the following Christmas?

Jessica was grateful for the distraction of Grant's return. After checking on his mother, he relieved Jessica on the stall and she took the opportunity to have a better look around the Hall herself, just in case she had missed anything she would need for her write-up.

Walking through to the entrance corridor, she noticed that Santa's Grotto was shutting up shop and Santa himself was at that moment headed out of the door. Ealisaid's sister Mairead was just inside the front room, picking up torn wrapping paper, no doubt dropped by over-excited children who had opened their Santa gifts on the spot.

Jessica moved over the speak to her. "Hi Mairead. How was your evening?" she asked, stepping through the door.

Inside the room, the grotto had been constructed from cardboard boxes, painted to look like a brick wall with a roaring fireplace. A second elf – Jessica recognized her as Katie, a friend of Mairead's from school – stood just in front of it, counting the leftover gifts and packing them into boxes.

Mairead turned and looked at Jessica. She was the double of her older sister, pale skin, and long dark silky hair which normally hung loose, parted in the middle, but today had been twisted into two plaits which had somehow – wire, perhaps? – been arranged so that that they turned upwards. Mairead had added exaggerated rosy red cheeks and a sprinkle of very deliberate freckles across her nose. Her green eyes looked especially vivid alongside the bright green of the tunic and leggings that she was wearing.

"Aye, OK I suppose. The kids came in, and only one or two burst oot greeting – crying. Santa did the job and then away he went." Mairead was never usually overly talkative, and nothing was different this evening, it appeared.

"I thought he was good this year," Katie piped up. "He kept quiet and let the kids chat away, and tell him what they wanted. They liked that, most of them! Some are just terrified from the start."

"So that's it all over? Isn't Santa coming back?"

Mairead gave her customary shrug, but her companion answered. "No. He's away to the pub, most likely – that's where he usually heads. Although he went off still in his Santa gear this year. I hope he took the back road or it'll take him a long time to get there – he'll be plagued by any children that are still up and aboot!"

Jessica was slightly disappointed. She had hoped to see the grotto in action, perhaps watch a bit of gift giving from the back of the room, but it probably didn't matter. Magnus had been there earlier and got photographs, so not much would be needed apart from a short caption.

"That's us done," Katie remarked, rubbing her hands. The room was neat, gifts stacked in boxes and not a shred of paper laying around. "I'm away home wi' my dad, Mairead. How're you getting back? We could give you a lift if you like."

"It's ok. My sister's coming to get me in a bit when the café closes. I'll stay here and help wi' clearing up in the big hall. See you Monday?"

"Aye, see you then!"

That might have been the most she had ever heard Mairead say, Jessica reflected. She walked together in silence with the young woman back to the main hall where everything was likewise winding up. Grant had already cleared his stall and packed away the remaining diaries and calendars.

True to her word, Ealisaid arrived about fifteen minutes later. She waved to Jessica and approached across the main hall as Mairead disappeared to pick up her bag and coat.

"How was your evening?" asked Jessica. "Rushed off your feet?"

"Absolutely fine. Not a drop of hot chocolate left, and I've got takers for all the Christmas cakes now. Reenie was closing up when I left, and she seemed to have done a roaring trade too. A successful wee Yule Night all round."

Jessica was pleased for both of them. Running a small business was never easy. At that moment, Ealisaid's phone pinged. She took it out and glanced at it. "It's Craig. I wonder what he wants." Ealisaid's friend Craig worked behind the bar at The Ram's Heid, and would therefore be working for some hours yet. Friday nights were never quiet, and with families all out and about for Yule Night, the bar had been buzzing – probably the busiest night of the year.

Jessica watched Ealisaid's brow furrow as she read the text. "What is it?" she asked, and – as her friend didn't reply – "is everything OK, Ealisaid?"

Ealisaid had paled. She looked up slowly and her eyes met Jessica's. "It's Bill Johnston – Santa. Craig says he found him in the cleaning cupboard up at the pub. Dead. It looks as if he's been murdered!"

The Morning After The Night Before

Despite having been amongst the first to receive the shocking news, neither Ealisaid nor Jessica had been able to do anything to help.

Ealisaid had to take Mairead home, but had first called Craig. He couldn't talk – there was too much to sort out with the police at the pub. Jessica had gone home as planned, but she knew that Ealisaid would be terribly worried about her friend. She also knew that Murdo would soon be pulled away on Special Constable business, meaning that Ealisaid and Mairead would be managing the café alone on a busy weekend before Christmas.

The next morning, Jessica and Reenie chatted quietly as they made their way to The Bloom Room, taking their usual route through the park. Reenie had been in bed when Jessica got home the night before so it had been breakfast time before she heard the news. They had talked about nothing but the murder since then. Now Reenie said again, "what a horrible end to a lovely, Christmassy evening. I wonder what on earth can have happened? The poor man."

The dirt paths in the park were hard underfoot, and the morning sun sparkled on the frost. Willow, their springer spaniel puppy, quite unconcerned by their sombre conversation, tried to investigate every white-coated blade of grass by the side of the path as they walked, and every partially frozen leaf. *They must have a different scent in the winter* thought Jessica, allowing the small dog a good sniff at the end of the leash before encouraging her on. It was too cold to stand about for long.

"Poor Craig, too," added Reenie. "It must have been a terrible shock for the lad."

Jessica nodded, hoping that the shock of finding Santa stuffed in the cupboard would be all that Craig had to endure, but she was certain he was in for some lengthy questioning as well. It's never good to be the person to discover a body, as she and her aunt had discovered earlier in the year. Craig surely wouldn't be implicated, however. The pub had been busy, and everyone knew exactly where Bill Johnston had been all evening. Besides, he must have been very distinctive when he turned up at the pub in his bright red suit. With that in mind, Jessica didn't see how much mystery there could be about this case. Surely there must have been plenty of witnesses? She would have to speak to Craig and find out. The sooner it was all sorted, the better. Jessica didn't want anything to spoil her perfect Scottish Christmas.

"Do you agree, Jessica?"

Distracted by her musings, Jessica hadn't been listening to her aunt.

"Sorry Reenie, could you repeat that? I was miles away."

Reenie looked at her, concern plainly visible on her face.

"I was saying, try not to get caught up in investigating anything. Leave this one to the professionals! The police will sort it out. It's their job, after all."

Jessica felt fairly sure there would be no need for her involvement, but she still wanted to know what was happening.

She found herself wondering whether Bill Johnston had any enemies; if, as according to Murdo, he was well known as a local curmudgeon then they would certainly have a starting point. She didn't say any of this to Reenie, instead replying: "I hope they get to the bottom of it soon – especially as it's almost Christmas. It would be awful if it dragged on."

Jessica became distracted by Willow pulling on the leash again, trying to get ahead more quickly. The puppy was certainly much better at walking now, but still occasionally would get overexcited and try to pull away, especially when she saw another dog – which was the case right now. This time however, Jessica successfully called her to heel and the puppy dropped back. Jessica reached down and fondled Willow's silky ears.

"Are you coming into the shop with me, Jess?" Reenie asked.

"Yes, I'd like to. I'm going to write up the Yule Night notes in the office later, but I'm not in a great hurry. I'd be happy to help you open up."

Jessica loved working for *The Herald,* and until recently had enjoyed working in the newspaper offices as well. They formed part of the first floor of a building adjacent to the Village Hall, above the library and beside a small, volunteer-run museum – a lovely setting. However, the recent cold snap had made her realize how hard it could be to heat old, stone buildings – she was finding it very chilly to work for long shifts at the office's computers. She had left her old, heavy laptop at home when she came to Scotland, given that it had originally been planned as a short trip. Jessica now regretted this decision. In principle, she could do most of her journalism work from anywhere – and right now would choose to find somewhere much warmer. Like at home, in front of Reenie's log fire.

She had started saving for a new laptop, but it was slow going.

The job was part-time and she had insisted on paying Reenie some money for rent and keep, although her aunt regularly protested that she didn't really need to. However, Jessica knew that it was Reenie's first year in business, and didn't want to take advantage of her good nature. She also didn't want her parents to help out more than they already had, and was determined to support herself as much as she could.

The laptop would have to wait. There was nothing for it but to do her work in short, efficient bursts until the weather warmed up again.

Reenie was replying: "That would actually be very helpful, as I have that christening tomorrow, remember? We can go over the arrangements and how I think I'd like to set it up. Are you still free to help me out with that?"

Jessica nodded. "Yes, I'm looking forward to seeing the hotel. I'll get the writing done today, and then I'm all yours tomorrow." The following day was a Sunday, and The Bloom Room had been booked to do the flowers for The Lochside Hydro hotel and country estate, somewhere out in the countryside near Dalkinchie. It was a popular high-end venue for all sorts of events including weddings and could potentially be a great source of business for the future.

"Perfect," said Reenie. "Maybe I'll treat you to a coffee afterwards at the hotel."

"I'd love that, sounds amazing."

The two women had turned from the park into the small street that led up to the middle of Dalkinchie High Street. As they neared The Bloom Room, they passed Malcolm McEwen, setting up his newspaper stand outside his grocery shop next door.

"Morning Reenie, Jessica."

Despite a rocky start, Reenie had become quite fond of her High Street neighbor who might have a gruff exterior, but could be very helpful when the occasion demanded.

"Morning, Malcolm. Don't worry, I haven't forgotten about the Business Association auction – I know you are going to ask me about it! I'll get something sorted soon."

"Aye, well, glad to hear that, although it's no' my problem any more, have you not heard? I've stepped doon as Chair of the Association since Thursday's committee meeting. It's yon Neil Campbell noo – he's got the stables on the way oot of the village. Speak to Neil aboot the auction, it's aff my hands – although knowing Neil, he'll probably find you first! But I'll be seeing you at the Cheese and Wine evening?"

Reenie smiled as she turned her key in the lock next door.

"You will indeed, Malcolm, I wouldn't miss it. Looking forward to seeing you and Sarah there."

Malcolm McEwen nodded and went inside his shop.

* * *

Having agreed to help Reenie in the morning, it was a couple of hours later by the time Jessica arrived at *Lissa's,* and as luck would have it, Craig was already there when she entered. His normally cheerful expression was absent, and his pale face spoke of stress and not much sleep. He sat hunched over a steaming mug at a table at the front of the café. Ealisaid was behind the counter as usual, and Mairead was on waitress duty, serving food – mostly breakfast rolls at this time of day – and clearing empty tables. Murdo, as Jessica had predicted, was absent.

Despite the events of the previous evening, the atmosphere

in Lissa's seemed very much the same as usual, although Jessica was sure that the murder would be the hot topic on everybody's lips. There was the usual crowd of elderly ladies spread around a couple of tables that they had pushed together, and they were enjoying a variety of cakes with their morning tea and coffee. Some local young parents had commandeered the space at the back of the café, a better position for them to store their push chairs. Both of Ealisaid's available highchairs had been pressed into service, and a couple of pre-school aged children played with the few toys that she kept in a box at the back for that purpose. Ealisaid's establishment was the heart of the community, and Jessica never failed to be impressed at the cozy feel she had created. Music played over the speakers – Christmas songs, of course.

"Morning Jessica, take a seat and I'll bring over your breakfast in a minute," Ealisaid said with a smile. Jessica was a regular now, but her friend would know that her visit today was as much to do with her need to know what was going on as it was about delaying the inevitable chilly shift in the newspaper offices.

Jessica began to reply, and as she did so realized that Ealisaid was telegraphing to her with raised eyebrows, jerking her head sharply towards the table near the front where Craig currently sat alone, staring at nothing at all. Jessica nodded to let her know she had got the message. Perfect. She had wanted to speak to Craig anyway, and moved over to his table. "Hi, Craig. I hope you're doing well this morning. Would it be all right if I joined you?"

"Hmm?" Craig had clearly been miles away. He shook his head slightly and looked at Jessica for a moment blankly, then – clearly realizing where he was – he nodded and attempted a smile. "Of course, Jessica, sit yourself down. It'll be nice to have the company." His actions belied his words however, as he resumed staring into space. This was very unlike him.

Jessica rushed to relieve the awkwardness with conversation. Feeling it was a little early to ask about the murder, she cast about for a neutral subject and settled on the news she had just heard.

"Have you heard about the new Business Association Chair? Malcolm McEwen was telling Reenie and me about him this morning. Someone called Neil Campbell?"

Once again it took Craig a moment or two to hear her, but when he did he clearly made an effort to reply.

"Oh aye…aye. Runs stables or something, so he does. I dinnae know him very well but he already got me to make a donation to the auction they're having so he's definitely on the ball." Craig fell silent again.

At this moment, Ealisaid brought Jessica's food and coffee over and took a seat herself, immediately breaking through the awkwardness of the situation. "So Craig, what's on the agenda today?" Ealisaid asked. "Have you got to open up the pub or will it stay shut for now?"

"Well, I don't actually know. I'm waiting here to have another chat with the polis."

Jessica noticed his particularly Scottish way of pronouncing this, with the emphasis on the first syllable. *Po-liss.* She knew Craig came originally from Glasgow, and was beginning to notice differences between Scottish accents from different cities and areas.

Craig continued. "They asked to meet me here. I think they'll find somewhere to hold some kind of formal interview. I'll maybe be able to open up tonight, no' sure yet – I hope so, the owner willnae be happy if I cannae open on a Saturday night in December. There will be people wanting to come in after the work nights oot, as well as the usual weekend crowd. One of the busiest nights of the year – and I've extra staff booked to come in too, like last night."

Jessica wondered if that would hold true once word got around. Dalkinchie was a small place, and there wasn't really anywhere else to socialize in the evening once *Lissa's* closed, apart from Gillespies. Would a murder put people off their weekend plans?

"Weren't you interviewed by the police last night?" Jessica asked.

Craig seemed to suddenly remember about his drink, and took a couple of large gulps before replying. "No. It was just sorting everything out, getting the ambulance. They asked me a couple of questions, but not a formal interview, so they said. They had to get a list of everyone who was there before I forgot, and I helped to do that. And they also wanted to know roughly what time Bill Johnston arrived, of course, and who was at the bar when he did, that sort of stuff."

"Right."

"But I expect I'll have to go over it all again today. You'd think it wouldnae be hard, what with him in that big red suit and all. I remember him arriving – I'm sure everyone does. The bar wis pretty busy at that point, and he didnae come and queue for a drink. No, I think he wis chatting to someone. No' his brother, although he wis there too – he'd been there all evening, but he was at the other end of the bar. They don't speak, you know."

"Hmm," said Jessica, "I suppose it would have been pretty busy by that point?"

"I certainly had a wee rush of orders around that time. A

group all came in together, and I was back and forward pouring gins and whiskies. And when I next looked up, he wis away. Bill that is – Santa. No sign. And I didnae see him leave. It wisnae until I had to go into the back cupboard…" He sighed, and took another gulp from the mug, then shook his head slightly. "The funny thing is, I usually wouldnae have to, but somebody went and dropped a glass, and it shattered. You'd think that would happen all the time at a bar, but it's actually pretty unusual. So I went to get a dustpan and brush to sweep it all up and that's when I found him. All shoved into the cupboard, still in the red Santa suit."

Jessica shuddered. "That must have been an awful shock, Craig!"

"Aye, right enough. I think I just went into autopilot after that, to be honest. Got my phone, dialed 999. Didnae even think about how he'd ended up there or who might have done it. I still cannae believe it. Santa, deid, in my cupboard."

Craig paused for a moment. He rubbed his hand over his reddened eyes, and then down his stubbled jawline. Then he continued. "I realized it wis Bill soon enough, of course. Poor guy. Doesnae really matter how unpleasant he wis – naebody deserves that!"

"Did you think he was unpleasant, Craig?"

Jessica was genuinely curious, but her question came out more accusing than she had intended. Craig reacted nervously, as if he had spoken out of turn. "On, no' me – I mean, he wis just a regular in the pub like anyone else. I didnae have any beef with him at all. I mean that some other folk said he wisnae a very nice man. I couldnae really say, one way or another. He ordered his drinks, I served him, and that wis that."

Jessica nodded, but couldn't help noticing Ealisaid's reaction.

She hadn't said anything since her initial question, and was now looking at Craig strangely as if he had said something very surprising. But before Jessica could comment or otherwise react to this, the door opened and Murdo arrived, followed closely behind by Detective Inspector James Gordon.

The Detective Inspector was a tall man with neatly combed greying hair, piercing blue eyes and, often, a grim expression that possibly went with the job. He could not be more different to the genial Murdo who, even under these circumstances, smiled at his friends and greeted them warmly.

"Jessica, morning. How are ye doing today? Craig, all right there, pal?"

The Detective Inspector and Murdo made an odd pairing, but were learning to work together. Not quite bad cop/good cop, Jessica didn't think, but something close to it. Murdo's friendly chatter put people at ease and – largely inadvertently – encouraged them to talk. DI Gordon was quieter, and tended to employ a much more direct approach to discussions.

Now, DI Gordon nodded silently towards Craig and Jessica, and then crossed the cafe to stand in line at the counter for coffee. Murdo, however, came over to their table. "What a palaver, huh? That's no' what anyone wis needin', just before Christmas. Craig, we've sorted oot the Village Hall for interviews as usual, would you be able to come up wi' us noo?"

Craig didn't look at all reassured although Murdo couldn't have been friendlier. He replied with a choked "Aye..." followed by "I'll just..." and then he got up and headed towards the rest room.

Murdo sat down in Craig's vacated seat and spoke as if to himself. "Oh, dearie dearie me. An awfy business, right enough."

Jessica tipped her head to one side. Murdo was known

for being garrulous, and she had learned that if she listened and stayed silent, he would often keep talking. She knew she was being nosy, but told herself that she was just honing her journalistic instinct. After all, she might not be working on local news forever.

Murdo didn't disappoint. "Imagine Bill Johnston gettin' murdered in his Santa suit – strangled wi' his own beard and stuffed in the cleaner's cupboard!"

Now Jessica slightly regretted that journalistic impulse – that was a detail she could maybe have done without. It seemed Murdo regretted telling her as he glanced around the café and dropped his voice. "Maybe no' mention that to anybody, Jessica, I think it was one o' the details the Detective Inspector said no' to spread around..."

Murdo continued. "Bill Johnston has been Santa every year as long as I can remember. He wis a funny choice, like I said, no' exactly someone who would spring to mind when you think 'jolly'. Still, he wis actually very good at playing the part. His private life wis a different story."

"Did he have family?"

"Nae kids. And he wis divorced, too. Or maybe separated – I'm no' sure. Anyway, his wife – ex-wife, I should say– moved away from here a few years back. And then there's his brother, and no doubt a few cousins here and there."

Jessica looked around towards the restrooms, but Craig had not yet emerged. "Well, it's a terrible thing, and not what anyone wants at this time of year. Still, surely someone must have seen something? I am sure you and the DI will have the case solved in the next couple of days."

Murdo looked at her. "Aye, maybe so. I wouldnae want it to drag on and ruin everyone's Christmas. We will be talking to his brother first. Ian. Aye, there was no love lost between Bill and Ian Johnston. They're brothers, aye, but also business rivals. Both have their own wee electrician firms."

"Oh, right." Jessica recalled that Murdo had mentioned this the night before, when she had seen Ian Johnston in the cafe shouting at the small child.

"Aye, most recently they were competing for the new contract at the Hydro. They haven't spoken for years, apart from to argue. I hope we're wrong, but we know that Ian was definitely at the pub around the time that Santa was found."

As Murdo spoke, Craig reappeared from the restroom and stood awkwardly near the front door of the café. DI Gordon had collected the take out coffees and turned to signal that he was ready to leave. Murdo got slowly to his feet.

"Weel, nice chatting to you, Jessica. I'll maybe be seeing you later. Cheerio for now."

Jessica bid Murdo goodbye, but her thoughts were somewhere else. The memory of Ian Johnston's altercation with the small girl and her father the night before had brought to mind the young woman she had seen reprimanded later, by another wiry, grey-haired man. Both brothers were electricians...Jessica realized that it had been Bill Johnston, the victim himself, that had been out in the courtyard fixing the electrics before the MacNaughton gave his speech, and had told his assistant off afterwards. He must have gone back inside to put on his Santa suit, as it was just a few minutes before the procession had set off.

Just as Jessica thought this over, the same young woman entered Lissa's. She recognized her instantly – the long plait over one shoulder, and she was again wearing work overalls, with a dark waterproof jacket over the top. Jessica's eyes followed her across as she walked to counter and ordered a drink, handing over a tall metal cup to be filled with coffee.

"Morning, Amy," said Ealisaid briskly. "I hope everything's OK with you, after last night. It's a real shock to us all."

Ealisaid's tone was sympathetic, but Jessica didn't catch Amy's response which was short and mumbled. Ealisaid nodded. The young woman paid up, using coins fished from her jacket pocket, and left the café.

Jessica didn't think twice. She followed.

Mince Pies at the Museum

Amy had turned right after leaving the café, and headed up the hill in the direction of The Ram's Heid. She walked with a long stride and as she didn't want to run, it took Jessica a minute to catch up with her.

"Hey...hey, Amy, is it? I'm Jessica. Can I have a quick word?"

Amy didn't break her step, barely glancing at Jessica as she replied. Her voice was deep and raspy, as if she was fighting off a cold. "I know who you are. You work for the newspaper, and no, I don't want to talk to the press. No comment."

Jessica was briefly nonplussed. Nobody had ever said this to her before, although it was technically an accurate description. She did work for the press. Normally describing herself as a journalist gave her a warm glow, but now she rushed to contradict this idea, and to reassure the young woman. "No, no, I am not reporting on anything, don't worry! I wanted to ask you something, that's all. It's just that..."

Jessica broke off. It was harder than she had anticipated to bring up the event that she had witnessed the night before. But she decided just to go for it. "I saw you setting up the lights last night before the procession, and I also saw Bill Johnston – am I right? – coming out to help. The two of you were looking at the cables near the stage. Was he your boss?"

Amy didn't say anything for a moment, still walking towards the top of the High Street. Then she nodded. "Yes. I'm an apprentice to his electrician firm. I've been doing it for nearly two years, and I should be finished in a couple of months."

Jessica pressed on. "I couldn't help but notice that he said something harsh to you before he went back inside the pub. I wasn't close enough to hear what he said, but it looked really mean. I don't think he treated you very well, did he?"

Amy paused, staring straight ahead without looking around at Jessica, and narrowed her eyes slightly. This time her answer came quickly. "Look, I don't know what you think you saw, but you were mistaken. He was just telling me something, that's all. It wasn't *mean* or anything like that. He was in a hurry. He had to go and get dressed for the procession, and I had interrupted him to check on something, so maybe he was a bit short, but nothing like you describe. We had a job to do."

Amy's response was composed, but for some reason, it seemed off to Jessica. Perhaps it had been something about the way she avoided catching Jessica's eye...and she was almost too composed. Thinking back, Jessica wondered if she had been mistaken. But no – there had been no mistaking the shock and embarrassment on Amy's flushed face, or the screwed-up expression of disdain on Bill Johnston's. If only she had been a bit closer and had heard what he had actually said – an argument so soon before the man's murder could easily be relevant to the case. Jessica was sure her instincts were correct. She couldn't resist having another try.

"Are you sure?" Jessica asked, resuming walking as Amy did so too. "You did look quite upset, you know. I had heard from someone else that he was...you know – not always very nice. Apart from when he was playing Santa, of course. I promise, this won't go any further. I really wanted to check and see if you were OK last night, actually, but you'd gone before I got a chance."

Amy's face had a glow of pink again, and she chewed at her bottom lip. She still stared straight ahead as she continued with her long, loping stride. "Yes. I went home. And I told you, it was nothing. You made a mistake. I don't know why you are asking all these questions, anyway, if you are not planning to report on the case. You are not the police! Please leave me alone. If you really must ask someone questions, why don't you find Bill's wife. I bet she's got something to say about it all. And they've had proper arguments – not a stupid disagreement at work."

Despite herself, Jessica's ears pricked up. Arguments with his wife too? Hadn't Murdo said she no longer lived in Dalkinchie? Things were getting interesting. Eyes wide, she responded, "His wife? I thought they were divorced, and that she didn't live here any more. What did they argue about?"

Amy stopped for a moment, cleared her throat, and turned properly to face Jessica for the first time, a slight look of superiority in her pink face. "Separated, not divorced – although I think she would like to be. And that's one thing you have right – she moved away from Dalkinchie about four years ago."

Jessica was about to ask how she was meant to question her then, when Amy continued:

"But she's back. Back for Christmas. I saw her in Gillespies last night, with a crowd of her old friends – all snobby show-offs just like she is. So if you really want to speak to someone who didn't like Bill Johnston, you should speak to her. I'm going now. I have to try and work out what to do now. Bill may be dead but there's still lots of work to do, and customers I'll need to speak to. See you around."

Amy's last rejoinder was clipped, and she took off, striding faster to get ahead of Jessica who now slowly stopped walking.

What was she doing? Reenie had asked her not to get involved. She could try to fool herself that she just wanted to check that the young woman was OK, but really the mystery had caught her interest again.

She knew that it must have, because there was nothing more she wanted to do right now than to find Bill Johnston's wife and ask her some questions too. However, that was a non-starter. She knew nothing about her, apart from what she had just learned – that the woman had eaten in Gillespies the night before.

Plus, she had work to do. Jessica turned on her heel and headed back down the hill in the opposite direction. She had put it off for long enough. It was time to go to work and try and force her chilly hands to type up the events of Yule Night, omitting the murder, of course.

* * *

Luckily, Jessica was waylaid once again. The newspaper offices shared a floor with the Dalkinchie Museum, and it was open on a Saturday. It was staffed by volunteers, one of whom, Margaret Mustard, was manning the door as Jessica ascended the stairs.

"Good morning, Jessica! Can I interest you in a wee hot drink and a mince pie? I've made them fresh!"

Jessica knew that this invitation was partly a ruse to get her into the museum, where Margaret would first engage her in gossip and secondly count her as a visitor for the weekly statistics, but she was happy to comply. Margaret was wonderful at baking, and the building was somehow warmer on this side. Perhaps it was because there were fewer windows. Plus, she wasn't averse to some gossip herself.

"That would be so nice, Margaret, thanks!"

Jessica moved through the doorway into the museum, which was a hodge podge of memorabilia crammed into two interconnected rooms. There were mannequins dressed in old clothing, a wooden dresser crammed full of delicately patterned china cups, saucers and plates with fat-bellied teapots arranged along the top, bookshelves holding worn hardback volumes and every inch of wall space was covered in framed old photographs. From her position near the door Jessica could see that they mostly depicted street scenes from years gone by of Dalkinchie and the neighboring town Drummond, with horses and carts and women in long Victorian dresses. An old fire engine took up much of the available floor space, along with a treacherous looking pieces of old farm equipment. Jessica considered the newspaper offices to be cluttered, but they had nothing on the museum.

Margaret had bustled into their shared kitchen space to produce two mugs of tea. "It's a Christmas blend," she announced as she returned "so I've only added just a wee tiny dash of milk. I think you'll like it."

Margaret Mustard was a force of nature, a woman known for her capabilities and her involvement in almost every sphere of local influence. She acted as a part-time housekeeper for clan chief Gillespie MacNaughton, and Jessica thought that she really considered the kitchen in Castle Drummond to be her own domain. She volunteered on Saturdays for the museum, was very active in the local Women's Guild and the Church of Scotland, and knew everything that happened in Dalkinchie and further afield sooner than seemed possible. Jessica knew that she would soon hear Margaret's take on the events of the night before, but for a moment allowed the drifting steam from the tea to soothe and calm her. She closed her eyes and inhaled as Margaret bustled through again to serve the mince pies – which, it turned out, she had warmed through. The scent of cinnamon and candied peel mingled with the spices in the tea – cardamom, Jessica thought, and definitely ginger. She felt deliciously warm all of a sudden.

"There ye go, I hope you enjoy that. It's my own wee special take on mince pies, I top them wi' crumble mix, not pastry – see what you think."

Jessica took a small bite. Melt-in-the-mouth deliciousness. Margaret's baking never disappointed. She took a sip of tea.

"So, what about that awfy business last night then? I was quite overcome when I heard. After all these years of being Santa!" Margaret took her own big slurp of tea, and then wedged her mug onto the counter beside her, in amongst what looked like a couple of birds' nests complete with delicate eggs, and a stuffed pine marten. This enabled her to munch into her own mince pie using two hands.

Jessica wasn't quite sure what the longevity of Bill Johnston's role as Santa had to do with it, but she was getting used to Margaret's particular take on events. She agreed.

"It's terrible. I just can't believe it, and so close to Christmas. I keep thinking that surely someone must have seen something...he turned up at the pub in his Santa suit."

Margaret nodded. "Aye, that's a bit odd. He was a wee bit late getting into the cart last night, I did notice that. He maybe didnae have his coat in all the rush. He must have made quite the entrance, coming in wi' the beard and the hat "

Jessica nodded. So Margaret had been there too, and had picked up on the kerfuffle before the procession started.

"Did you see his assistant, Amy, there?"

Margaret paused and frowned, her sandy colored eyebrows knitting together above her bright eyes and rouged cheeks.

"I cannae mind…I wis at the back of the crowd, not near the front. I dinnae think I saw Amy. Was she working on the sound system? Did something happen? I saw Gillespie wis out for a wee while on the platform before he started speaking."

Jessica wasn't sure whether she should confide in Margaret or not, but she still had an inkling that Amy had been lying to her and wanted the full story. If anyone knew it, Margaret would.

"I thought I saw Bill Johnston being mean to her. He seemed to speak to her sharply and then she looked upset. I wasn't close enough to overhear or anything, but I was positive that she was near to tears. However, I just met her in the village and she said it was nothing, that I must have misunderstood."

Margaret had started nodding halfway through Jessica's tale, but having just taken another bite of mince pie, she wasn't able to answer straightaway.

"Oh, no doubt, no doubt. That sounds about right. A proper mean-spirited soul was Bill Johnston, and I don't care who hears me say that. He's more like Scrooge than Santa, but he's always done it – and his father before him – so nobody ever crossed him. Anyway, as for Amy. She's on a college apprenticeship with him, and I know the lassie, I knew her granny and she is doing fine, has always worked away hard and picked it up as she went. But she makes mistakes sometimes – who doesnae when they are learning – and he never lets her hear the end of it. In fact I did hear–"

Here Margaret broke off, leaned in closer and dropped her voice, perhaps in case there was anyone on the stairs or hiding behind one of the bookshelves that might overhear.

"– I heard he was about to fail her on her final assessment for the college, which would mean she would fail overall, and have to resit a year."

Margaret drew back, her eyes open, unblinking and fixed on Jessica's as she did a couple of long, slow nods to further emphasize her point. But she hadn't finished.

"And you know what that would mean, don't you?"

Jessica didn't, but couldn't help being drawn in by Margaret Mustard's dramatic telling of events.

"What?"

"Bill Johnston would get another year of paying her a pittance at apprenticeship wages."

Upon hearing this, Jessica had an inkling of why Amy had lied to her. She kept it to herself, nodding along as Margaret changed the subject to her neighbor's cat. They both finished their mince pies and tea, before Jessica thanked Margaret and excused herself to go next door to her own office.

The two rooms were even colder than usual if possible. Jessica turned on a small fan heater but it made little different to the chill that crept in through the large windows. She typed up her notes on the previous day as quickly as she could, grateful that the work was straightforward because her thoughts kept returning to the conversations she had just had with Margaret Mustard and with Amy the apprentice. She couldn't shake the picture of Amy's upset face of the night before from her mind.

Taken all together, this was the closest thing to a motive for Bill Johnston's murder she had heard yet.

The Lochside Hydro

"Oh, I wish it could be Christmas every day…" Reenie sang along as she drove, accompanied by the Christmas music playing loudly on the van's stereo system. She wouldn't win any prizes for singing, but her voice was loud, confident and held a tune.

Jessica joined in.

"Let the bells ring out for Christmas!"

It was Sunday morning, and Reenie and Jessica were making their way along the winding, country roads towards the Lochside Hydro. As usual, Reenie was driving her old rattly green van and as usual, Jessica wondered whether it would survive much longer. The heating had gone on it now, and Jessica was grateful for her thick coat, soft blanket scarf and the bobble hat she had pulled down right over her ears.

Reenie and her twin sister Bella, Jessica's mom, had told Jessica that she had spent Christmas in Scotland once before, as a small child. Jessica couldn't remember that, so was counting this one as her first. Would there be another in the years that followed? To anyone who asked, Jessica described her current situation as a year out – a chance to get some real journalism experience before deciding whether to return and take up her deferred place. As her whereabouts of the following year were looking uncertain, Jessica was viewing this Christmas as a chance to put the last one behind her, as well as possibly the only one she would spend in Dalkinchie. She was spending it with family and friends, people she loved, and she was determined that it would all go perfectly, down to every last detail. Solving a murder mystery was *not* a part of that, and Jessica had squashed her suspicions of the day before down firmly. Let Murdo and DI Gordon sort it out.

Her aunt interrupted her thoughts.

"It's not far now. I always remember to look for the turning after I've passed the Stables." Reenie waved to the left, where a large painted sign announced *Campbell's Stables and Livery*.

A few minutes later, Reenie drove through a wide, ornate entrance way, with signs pointing towards 'Reception', the 'Speyside Spa' and 'Highland Lodges'. Although this was Jessica's first visit, Reenie had been before, attending a wedding fayre hosted by the hotel. She had described the place as luxurious, and Jessica, looking through the van windows as Reenie expertly parked the vehicle near an entrance at the back of the complex, could see what she meant. The grounds were landscaped with neat shrubberies and clean, well-maintained paving. The walkways were decorated with small, real spruce trees in shiny red pots placed at even intervals along them.

The morning was dry, and Jessica could see that some people were taking advantage of the gardens, strolling amongst the frosted greenery. A tall woman, wearing a padded red coat with a fur hood, long shiny chestnut-colored boots and a snowy white fluffy scarf, walked arm in arm with a slightly shorter woman, who was equally well wrapped up in a navy wool coat and ear muffs over her thick, curly hair.

Reenie got out of the van.

"Let's make sure we have access to the room first, and know

where we're going before we start unloading."

Jessica nodded. They made their way towards the entrance, footsteps crunching over the gravel of the parking lot. As they drew close to the door, a man exited. He wasn't tall, but held himself with a very straight back. He had ruddy cheeks, dark reddish-blond hair and was wearing an expensive-looking checked tweed blazer. A soft, dark green woolen scarf was his only concession to the cold.

"Reenie Maguire? Owner of The Bloom Room?" He tucked the files he was carrying under his left arm so that he could shake Reenie's hand. "Neil Campbell, Campbell's Stables. I'm the new Business Association Chair. Nice to meet you properly, I've been hoping to catch up with you. I would have popped in yesterday evening, but I'm afraid I was laid up with a bad cold."

Reenie shook the man's hand. "Lovely to meet you too, Neil, although I'm in a bit of a hurry –"

"Oh, I won't keep you long, I was just hoping you could confirm the details of your donation to our charity auction, which we'll be holding on the same evening as the Business Association Christmas Cheese and Wine." Neil Campbell was smiling but also unmoving, slightly blocking the entrance way – not entirely accidentally, Jessica felt.

Jessica, knowing her aunt well, could sense her impatience but Reenie replied as pleasantly as she could.

"Yes, of course. I had already said to Malcolm I would donate, when he was Chair. It will be a Christmas centerpiece arrangement, or another arrangement of equivalent value. Would you like me to make up a gift voucher?"

"I would. I will come in and pick it up this week." Still smiling, Neil Campbell turned to Jessica.

"Jessica Greer, I believe? Do you think the *The Drummond*

and Dalkinchie Herald would be willing to make a donation as well? I was thinking perhaps a photoshoot, or something along those lines."

Jessica couldn't help but be a little impressed at the man's audacity. He might put people's backs up, but he would certainly make a good Chair.

"Our photographer works freelance, and I'm only a junior reporter, so couldn't promise anything else. I'll tell Grant you asked, though."

Neil Campbell nodded and stepped a little to one side to allow Reenie and Jessica access to the hotel. His expression hadn't changed. He moved off towards his car – a highly polished gunmetal grey Range Rover with a personalized number plate that read 'NE17 CAM'. Reenie waited until they were out of earshot before muttering her opinion to Jessica.

"He's the polar opposite of Malcolm, isn't he – very flashy! And a bit pushy for me, too."

Reenie and Jessica carried the flowers through carpeted corridors to the event room where the christening was taking place. Reenie had made up most of the arrangements the day before, leaving only a few last minute touches for this morning. The christening ceremony was taking place in a nearby church, followed by this formal lunch at the Lochside Hydro. Jessica counted ten round tables, each of which was to receive a floral centerpiece. Two larger arrangements were placed on stands near the front of the room, flanking a covered table which would bear the cake.

As they moved in and out of the hotel, carrying the centerpieces carefully one-by-one, the room grew more and more beautiful. Jessica marveled at Reenie's ability to produce arrangements that perfectly acknowledged the season, while still not being too full-on Christmassy. After placing the final touches to the room, Reenie snapped a quick photograph on her phone. She pocketed it and rubbed her hands together, smiling in pleasure.

"Well, that's a job well done, I think."

Jessica gazed at the room.

The color scheme was deep pink, dark green and frosted silver which twinkled under the chandeliers. The proportions of the centerpieces were perfectly balanced across the tables, and their delicate mix of flowers echoed the more elaborate arrangements at the front. It all looked simply magical.

"I'm done now, but I would like one of the events staff just to look in and check it over. Do you mind if we have a look for someone?"

Jessica knew that Reenie would want the events manager to see her handiwork, in the hope that she might be recommended for future work. They decided to have a wander through the hotel, and to treat themselves to a coffee in the hotel bar before heading home. Reenie had invited Grant for Sunday lunch so it would soon be time to get started on that, but there was always time for a coffee.

As luck would have it, Reenie didn't have to look far. As soon as they rounded the bend in one of the corridors, they saw one of the staff in conversation with another man – a man that Jessica recognized. The shock of gray hair and his hunched gait gave him away as Ian Johnston. Just like the previous occasion, he seemed to be having an altercation. The pair were still a distance away from Reenie and Jessica, and not wanting to intrude or seem to eavesdrop, they awkwardly slowed to a halt. Reenie didn't want to leave either, and miss her chance to make a good first impression.

The two women couldn't hear what was being said, but it was obvious from the demeanor of the two men and the hotel worker's gesticulations that something was off. Ian Johnston waved his arm and stomped off. The hotel worker paused and visibly took a deep breath before moving on, walking in the opposite direction to Ian Johnston and therefore down the corridor towards Reenie and Jessica.

Now smiling, he came forward to greet Reenie. His name badge proclaimed him to be Stuart McKillop, Manager.

"Are you the florist? I've been waiting to have a word with you. The Glenmorangie Suite looks spectacular!"

As Reenie chatted to Stuart, Jessica looked around at her surroundings. They were in an open area within the hotel complex, with further corridors leading to rooms and more event spaces, and a sign pointing towards the Lochside Hydro's various dining venues. Above a small tartan padded chair there was a large framed history of the hotel. Jessica read about its beginnings as a Hydropathic Spa in the Victoria era, part of a number of Scottish hotels who popularized nature and water cures, based on an Edinburgh doctor's experience of spas in Eastern Europe. She learned that it had housed Polish soldiers during the Second World War, and had been a dry establishment until relatively recently – only beginning to serve alcohol towards the end of the 20th century. Even after six months in Scotland, Jessica was still amazed at the way that every building had history attached, and how much the other people around her took it for granted. She took every opportunity she could to learn more about the country and the cities, towns and buildings within it.

Reenie finished her conversation with Stuart and he moved on down the corridor. Beaming, she turned to Jessica.

"Well, he definitely likes my work! Let's hope he tells lots of people about my business. I think a little celebration is in order. We'll go and have that cuppa in the Lochside Bar before we head back home and I need to put the oven on."

The Lochside Bar was not particularly busy at this hour on a Sunday morning. Reenie found them a cozy little table in the corner, beside a window which overlooked the loch. As her aunt went to the bar to order drinks, Jessica enjoyed the scenery – a wide sweep of lawn, running down to the water's edge, with groups of trees dotted here and there. Everything was still and blanketed in frost, the perfect winter landscape.

Reenie returned with their coffees. Her own was her standard black coffee, but Jessica had fully embraced the seasonal mood, ordering a latte with gingerbread flavored syrup, topped with whipped cream, sprinkled nuts and the tiniest, cutest little gingerbread elf.

As Reenie and Jessica sat and relaxed, a familiar looking woman entered the bar. Jessica realized that she had seen her walking outside in the grounds when they first arrived. The woman stood at the entrance for a moment, scanning the room, and spotting them at their table, made her way over. She had discarded the red padded coat she had been wearing earlier and now simply wore her skinny jeans with the shiny chestnut boots and a beautiful dark green sweater. As she drew closer, Jessica also spotted the expensive looking sparkling earrings she wore, and a fine gold chain around her neck.

It was obvious she was coming to speak to them, and Reenie greeted the woman as she arrived at their table. She was holding a business card in her hand, turning it over in her fingers as she moved across the room, and Jessica saw Reenie's own distinctive 'TBR' logo on it.

"Hi. I hope you don't mind me interrupting you. I was just speaking to Stuart, the manager here. He told me that you did the flowers that I saw on the way in."

Reenie stood up and offered her hand.

The woman shook it and went on, introducing herself. "I'm Samantha Johnston. I'm not from around here any more, although I used to live locally. I am staying in the resort at the moment, and I couldn't help but notice your beautiful flowers and thought I must come and speak to you – you see, I might be in need of a florist soon."

As soon as Jessica had heard the woman speak her name, she knew who she must be – and in fact, she now realized, she had seen her before, in the window of Gillespies on the night of the procession. Flowers? She wondered if Samantha Johnston would have to organize the funeral, and the thoughts went through her brain all at once. If she was still Bill Johnston's next of kin –and as his wife, separated or not, she probably would be – then it the arrangements probably would fall to her.

Jessica hoped that Reenie would make the connection too, but she needn't have worried. Her aunt was far too professional to make any assumptions about the nature of the event. "Of course. My business, The Bloom Room, has a shop in Dalkinchie High Street. It's best to talk in person, but if that isn't convenient for you, then we can speak over the phone, or communicate via email."

Reenie nodded towards the card in Samantha Johnston's hand.

"Can I have a quick word with you just now, perhaps?"

Samantha Johnston pulled over a chair from a neighboring table and perched on the edge of it, crossing her legs as she did so. She looked inquiringly at Reenie.

Reenie glanced at Jessica, who nodded a little. She knew her aunt well, and knew that Reenie was keen to secure this business, but would also feel guilty about interrupting their morning coffee. Jessica didn't mind. She was happily enjoying her gingerbread latte, looking at the window and, if she happened to overhear any gossip from Samantha Johnston, that could hardly be her fault now, could it?

Reenie answered.

"Of course. I'd be happy to have a chat with you just now, but a more in-depth discussion, it really would be better if you would be able to come to the shop and see what I have."

A small flicker of something like annoyance crossed Samantha Johnson's face. She made a vague handwaving gesture, as if to brush away Reenie's suggestion. She replied:

"I've seen what you have, in the function suite. I'm sure you can do a good job. I was thinking, maybe, roses and tulips..."

Reenie nodded. She answered as best she could:

"Tulips, and roses to some extent, are best suited to happy, celebratory occasions. For funerals and sympathy arrangements I would usually suggest lilies made up with carnations and chrysanthemums, although roses can also do well if you like them, and I'm happy to source and incorporate whatever our customers want. In addition, while tulips are available all year round, the prices are definitely seasonal, and they are very expensive right now. I can understand if you'd rather not talk about this now, but it really helps if you have an idea of budget from the outset. If there's some time pressure..."

Jessica watched Samantha Johnston's face as her aunt spoke. Her expression didn't change, but she tilted her head very slightly to one side, as if considering Reenie's words.

"I'm not worried about budget. I hadn't considered the

suitability aspect though, and you are right, I probably should take a look at what you can do. I'll take your advice and pop into the shop. In the High Street you say?"

"Yes, number twelve." Reenie replied.

"Great. I'll see you there sometime this week. Thanks for your help."

Samantha Johnston swung her curtain of shiny blonde hair around her back, and stood up, leaving the chair she had displaced exactly where it was. She nodded to both Reenie and Jessica, and left, walking back across the bar to where Jessica could see her companion, the woman from earlier, was waiting at the entrance. Reenie waited until they had completely left the bar before saying in quiet tones to Jessica:

"Did I handle that really badly? I didn't want to let her know that I knew who she was, and knew that she was probably arranging a funeral. I tried to talk in the most general terms, but I think I might have put her off. I mean, if she wants tulips, she can have tulips..."

Jessica, still looking over to where the couple had left, wasn't sure. She felt that Reenie's words had been entirely appropriate, but there was no denying that Samantha Johnston had reacted oddly. Almost as if they had been talking at cross-purposes. She tried to reassure her aunt.

"I'm sure it was nothing you said, Reenie. If she wants your flowers, she'll be back. She must be under a lot of stress."

Although even as she said this, Jessica thought that if Samantha Johnston *was* under a lot of stress, she wasn't showing it. Despite herself, Jessica felt her curiosity piqued again.

* * *

Jessica and Reenie returned to the cottage, where Reenie immediately began preparations for a roast chicken dinner. One of the wonderful things about Dalkinchie was the availability of fresh local produce, and in this instance Reenie had bought the chicken from the local butcher who also sold vegetables directly supplied by local farms. Jessica scrubbed potatoes that had been grown in the lush fields that lay between Dalkinchie and Drummond, and moved on to peel carrots that had come from one of the local smallholdings managed by the Drummond estate.

"Right, Jessica. You are on the veg, I'm doing some Yorkshire pudding to go with it. I think I'll make your granny's homemade gravy recipe, and also fry up some skirlie." Reenie was a good cook, although her long hours meant that during the week she usually relied on quick and simple dishes.

"Skirlie? What's that?" If Jessica had eaten skirlie before, she didn't remember.

"Oatmeal and onions fried in butter. It's delicious. See what you think when you taste it." As Reenie spoke, she placed three large apples on a baking tray. Stuffed with raisins, butter and cinnamon, the apples went into the oven. Reenie, aware of the feasting to come, planned these as a lighter option – but given that she would serve the warm, spiced fruit with heavy cream from Balnaguise, the Smiths' dairy farm, Jessica was certain that it wouldn't turn out to be all that light after all.

Grant arrived promptly at one o'clock, bearing a bottle of wine and some oatcakes. Jessica answered the door.

"Hi, Grant! How are you?"

"I'm well, and glad to be here! It suits me perfectly. My mother is at a senior Christmas lunch in the Village Hall, so it's nice not to be cooking for one."

Jessica smiled as she took his coat, keeping her thoughts to herself.

He had brought his black labrador, Skye, with him, and Jessica was entertained as always by Willow's reaction. The little dog had been lurking in the kitchen, hyper-aware of all the delicious smells, but as soon as the dignified older dog arrived she fell into her usual habit of pestering her. Skye stood patiently, her tail gently waving as the puppy capered around her, letting out two short barks. Then the labrador walked to her usual spot in front of Reenie's fire and, after a good scratch, curled up in Willow's bed, which was comically too small for her. Willow seemed slightly confused by this, sniffing around Skye and then sitting. After this, she lay down with her head resting on her front paws, watching Skye. The labrador ignored her, and closed her eyes.

Grant had moved into the open-plan kitchen and fallen immediately into a rhythm of working with Reenie that Jessica had observed before. Although Reenie had only met Grant for the first time when she moved from Edinburgh to Dalkinchie earlier that year, this easy familiarity and connection between them had arisen almost immediately. Jessica knew that both of them had their challenges – Reenie was focused on building up her new business and her new life away from the city, and Grant's caring responsibilities and full-time job meant he didn't have much time to himself – but she felt that this should not present a barrier if the two of them wanted to be together. Now she watched as the timer went off, and Grant automatically passed Reenie the oven mitts.

"Lunch is ready!"

Reenie carried through warmed plates, followed by platters of vegetables, roast potatoes and Yorkshire pudding. Grant was carving the chicken.

Jessica had been relegated to setting the table when Grant arrived, aware that three people in Reenie's compact kitchen was one too many. Now as they took their seats around the table Jessica reflected once again on the way that this had become the norm, and how comfortable she felt sitting and eating with her Scottish 'family'. With the cooking finished and all fans and rings switched off, Reenie's kitchen radio could be heard. On Sunday afternoons there was always a show featuring musical hits presented by a famous singer, and for Jessica, who loved musicals, it added to the festive feel.

For a few minutes all the conversation related to the meal.

"Pass the gravy please, Jessica."

"Grant, would you like more roast potatoes?"

"Does anyone want extra chicken?"

There was then a prolonged silence as everyone tucked in. After about five minutes, the conversation picked up again. Grant and Jessica never wanted to bore Reenie with work talk so saved it for their own meetings. This meant that today there was only one topic – the murder of Bill Johnston on Friday night.

"It's a tragic business, of course, but it's also quite an extraordinary tale. The Ram's Heid is not a particularly large building, and I can't help but feel that whatever happened must have been visible to bystanders. The pub was probably at its busiest just after the village festivities wound up, with those coming in from the cold joining those who had been there all evening. I suppose the rush must have kept Craig busy, but someone must have seen something?"

Grant paused to take another mouthful of chicken, gravy and Yorkshire pudding. Jessica interjected.

"That's exactly what I've been saying! You're right, Grant

– Craig says a crowd came in just after Bill did, and he was distracted by serving them. When he next looked up, Bill was nowhere to be seen. But the pub was full of people. So I just don't see how it could have happened without being noticed."

Grant nodded, taking a sip of his wine before continuing. "I've been wondering about his young apprentice too, Amy Matthews," he said. "She's a nice girl, but quite reserved and aloof. I hope she's OK. I don't know what this will mean for her work, and I hope she has someone to talk to about things."

Jessica replied, eager to share what she had observed about Amy. "Actually, I spoke to her yesterday about it. You see, I thought – no, I am sure – that Bill upset her on Friday night just before the procession started. I didn't realize it was him at the time, but she was trying to get the sound system working and couldn't, and had to go in and ask for help. I suppose he was probably getting dressed up as Santa at the time but he had to stop and come out to fix whatever it was. He definitely had a word with her before he went back inside, and she was upset. However when I asked her yesterday she just denied it. In fact, she told me that I should be talking to his wife, and that they had argued." As she said this, Jessica began to wonder what exactly that argument had been about. Grant started to reply.

"Ah, yes…"

He didn't get any further before Reenie interrupted. "Jessica, I thought you weren't going to focus on anything to do with the case. I thought we agreed you shouldn't get involved this time?"

Jessica turned in surprise to look at her aunt, who rarely spoke crossly. She hadn't raised her voice, but it was apparent from the shake in it that she was upset.

"I know Reenie, but it was nothing much. I had just seen

Amy on Friday and when I spotted her in the café yesterday it seemed to make sense to follow her out and–"

"You followed her out? Jessica, why would you do that? It's none of your business why she was upset!"

Grant looked from Reenie to Jessica, and then looked down, clearly not wishing to get involved. Jessica felt defensive, as well as slightly panicky. She really didn't want to fall out with her aunt – not at all, but definitely not this close to Christmas. *Please, I just want everything to go smoothly!*

"Well, I didn't think anyone else had seen and I just wanted to help her – and perhaps figure out what was going on. I think she might have a point Reenie – didn't you think Samantha Johnston behaved a bit oddly this morning?"

Reenie did raise her voice now.

"I didn't think anything of the sort. I was speaking to her only as a potential client, and it wouldn't have been appropriate for me to think of her in any other way. Are you actually saying that you think that she was involved in her ex-husband's murder?"

"Well, no, I don't know, I just thought –"

Grant stood up.

"Excuse me ladies, I'll just go and get some…" He drifted off, clearly wanting to escape to the kitchen so that he didn't have to be involved in their argument. Jessica felt a momentary pang of guilt. Reenie continued.

"Jessica, I have already said that you should not be getting involved in this. I am concerned for your safety, and I have said to your parents that I would make sure you didn't put yourself at risk again. You told me that you wouldn't investigate, and I would appreciate it if you would stick to your word. I am responsible for you while you live here with me."

Jessica's emotions were a confusion of guilt, empathy for

Reenie's point of view and annoyance at being spoken to as a child. Surely it was her decision whether she got involved or not? She opened her mouth to reply. "Reenie, I appreciate your concern, really I do, but I'm all grown up now. I won't take any risks."

She may as well not have spoken. Reenie continued without listening.

"You shouldn't be doing this, Jessica. It's the job of the police to find out who killed Bill Johnston, not yours. Running around asking questions, trying to figure things out...The police don't need you interfering."

Sleuthing

"Jessica, your help would be very much appreciated."

DI Gordon spoke decisively, and Murdo nodded along. The two policemen had established themselves in their usual temporary office in one of the Village Hall's smaller rooms.

It was Monday, and Jessica hadn't spoken to Reenie that morning. Yesterday's meal had finished awkwardly, a stilted silence broken occasionally by Grant's attempts at making conversation. Jessica cleaned up while Reenie and Grant took the dogs for a walk together, and when Reenie returned Jessica busied herself by tidying out her room, and doing some laundry for the week ahead.

They had each, separately, made themselves a quick sandwich with leftovers in the evening and then Reenie went for an early night. This wasn't unusual – it was the Perth flower market on Monday, and it started very early – but Jessica couldn't help but feel that the tension from their argument lay unresolved. Reenie and Willow were out of the cottage early, long before Jessica woke up on Monday. She had skipped breakfast at home, proceeding straight to *Lissa's* where she hoped to be able to unload on Ealisaid – but her friend had been too busy, so Jessica had breakfasted alone, before getting the message from Murdo inviting her to come up to the Village Hall for 'a wee chat.'

Now she stared at the Detective Inspector, unsure of what he had just asked. "You need my help…with the Bill Johnston case?"

DI Gordon replied.

"Yes. You may believe, as many do, that it can't be that hard to solve this one. Unfortunately, that's not what we are finding. I'm not going to share every detail, but suffice to say that we had enough information to begin building a case against a specific individual, and it's not entirely stacking up. We will continue to pursue it, but we do need some idea of alternatives. As you have shown yourself to be a very observant individual in the past, we wondered whether you had any thoughts. If this case drags on past Christmas –" The Detective Inspector didn't finish his sentence.

Jessica felt like she should feel smug, but she didn't. In fact, she felt really nervous. Perhaps Reenie had been right. After all, the previous cases she had been involved in had put her in real danger at times. On the other hand, she hated the thought of DI Gordon missing out on Christmas celebrations with his partner and the babies. He should be able to put this case behind him, relax and enjoy the special occasion, as should Murdo. She made up her mind.

"How can I know what will help if I don't know who your suspect is?"

DI Gordon sighed. He looked at Murdo, who shrugged as if in agreement with Jessica. "Very well then. We have ruled out Bill Johnston's ex-wife, who has an alibi for the whole evening. We have been examining Ian Johnston, Bill's brother. He was the obvious first suspect. He was in the pub that evening, and was certainly present when Bill Johnston arrived there after his Santa duties. It's well-known locally that the two brothers don't get on.

"Ian Johnston is also an electrician and in fact the two men were in business together, carrying on their father's business, 'Johnston and Sons'. There was a falling out between them about fifteen years ago, and they divided the business and both struck out on their own. Since then they haven't had much to do with each other, despite working in the same trade and living in the same village – and drinking in the same pub. There has been no outright animosity until recently."

The Detective Inspector paused. He looked at Murdo, who had been nodding as the Detective Inspector spoke, and now began to take up the tale.

"There wis a big contract going, see, at the Lochside Hydro – have you heard o' it?"

Jessica nodded.

"I was actually there just yesterday, helping my aunt set up for an event."

"Aye well, you'll have seen that they have a big fancy hotel and huge big gardens. They've also got posh lodges on the grounds, and an apartment block as well. The contract was for more o' the lodges. They're planning to build quite a few more over the next few years, so it will be guaranteed work for quite a while for lots of contractors. It's a great place, so it is. I've never stayed there –well, I wouldnae, that would be daft as it's just up the road – but I have been to a lovely wedding there, just beautiful it was. A friend o' mine from school, and one of the bridesmaids got in a right row wi' the mother o' the bride just before the cake cutting. I think they had both had a wee bit too much to drink, but they started this big argument aboot the bridesmaid's shoes, of all things."

DI Gordon took over again, cutting straight over Murdo. *I'll ask him about the bridesmaid's shoes later,* thought Jessica, who always enjoyed Murdo's asides.

"You can imagine that this contract would form a reasonable motive, Jessica. You see, while the brothers' animosity towards each other was well known, and they haven't worked together for years, it would be completely out of character for one of them to suddenly attack the other now. They have managed to co-exist in relative peace, so it would take a trigger – like competing for the same lucrative contract – to bring about a turn of events such as took place on Friday evening."

Jessica understood. She asked:

"So what's the situation? Why does this not stack up?"

DI Gordon took a moment to reply.

"The contract was awarded two weeks ago. To Ian Johnston, the surviving brother."

He paused to let that sink in, then continued.

"Why would Ian Johnston murder his brother now, having successfully bid for the contract? You might understand it if it was the other way around – but we have checked and double checked the facts over the weekend. Ian Johnston definitely won the Lochside Hydro contract. His quote was substantially cheaper. Bill Johnston lost out.

"If anyone had a motive for murder, it was Bill Johnston, not Ian."

Jessica reflected on this. She could understand the Detective Inspector's frustration. Ian Johnston had been in the pub when his brother arrived, and was known to dislike him. But it was very difficult to see what he might have to gain.

"So, Jessica, we thought we would ask if you had picked up anything else," said Murdo. "You've always got your nose in something and you always seem to have it figured oot before anyone else – have you seen or heard anything that might help us oot?"

Murdo looked earnestly at Jessica and she nodded. Well, it was true, she did know something, and she could hardly refuse a direct request to share information with the police, could she? She would explain to Reenie. It would be fine.

"Have you spoken to Bill Johnston's apprentice? Amy Matthews?"

DI Gordon was the first to reply.

"Only briefly, just to ascertain where she was on the night of the murder. She was the one that initially told us about the contract, actually, and then we verified it. Why?"

Jessica didn't like having to say the words out loud. Despite Amy's brusqueness, she didn't dislike the young woman and hated having to implicate her. However, facts were facts.

"I think she might have a motive too."

* * *

Back out in the street, Jessica reflected upon her assignment. DI Gordon and Murdo had agreed that Amy's situation required verifying, but were also wary to be seen chasing unsubstantiated gossip. They thought that the best approach was for Jessica to try and engage her again and see if anything Margaret Mustard had said was true.

Murdo had given her the address of the electrician's office, but when she found it tucked down a side street, it was closed up and the lights were off. There was no notice to inform potential customers about what to do. Jessica tried the door just in case – locked. She turned around.

Murdo had said that he thought that Amy lived in the flats –

apartments – opposite the shop and Jessica decided it was worth a try. She moved across the street and found a green doorway, flaking paint, adorned with a brass number four. Beside the door, fastened to the wall was a buzzer system with four buttons and a speaker grille. The buttons were numbered but that was it – no further identification and no obvious way to tell who might live there. Jessica took a deep breath and pressed the first one.

Nothing.

She gave it another, longer press and then counted slowly to twenty. Still nothing.

She pressed the second button and was about to repeat it again when there was a crackling noise and a wavery "Hullo…?"

"Hi there! I'm looking for Amy Matthews. Is this her place?"

"Amy? Aye, she lives in this close, hen, but you'd be better off pressing her buzzer. I don't know if she's in today."

Jessica tried to quickly ask which of the remaining two was the correct button, but it was too late, the woman had disconnected.

Deep sigh.

Jessica pressed the third button. This time the response was swifter – and unmistakably Amy's voice.

"Hello? Can I help you?"

"Hi! Amy? It's Jessica here…Jessica Greer. We spoke on the street?"

"Oh, yes. Hello. Well, come in then."

With that, the call was abruptly ended and a buzzing noise signaled the release of the lock on the door. Jessica pushed it slowly inward.

She entered into a dark corridor, with a door leading off on either side on the first floor. A voice called "up here!" and

Jessica climbed the concrete stairs to see that it was the same on the second floor – an entryway on either side. One of the doors – painted a cheerful bright blue – was ajar, and Jessica knocked it before pushing gently.

"Come in!"

Amy emerged into the hallway from a room, drying her hands. She was wearing jeans and a tartan shirt today, but was barefoot and her long hair was still damp. As Jessica watched, she twisted it into her long braid which then lay over her shoulder.

"Hi, Jessica. I'm glad you came round. I need a favor."

Jessica tried not to show her surprise. "What can I do for you?" Amy gestured for Jessica to follow her into a living room. It was slightly old-fashioned but very tidy, modern framed prints on the wallpapered walls incongruously hanging above the solid dark wood furniture, the large, well-padded velvety couches and thick carpet.

The sash windows were open, just a crack, although the day outside was brisk and cold. Amy went over and closed them before coming back over and perching on the arm of the sofa.

"I need to move this ottoman, and it's far too heavy for me to do on my own. Would you mind helping?" She motioned towards the window, and Jessica saw the upholstered box sitting underneath.

"Sure, no problem. Where is it going?" Perhaps if she helped, Amy would be more likely to open up to her.

"Into my bedroom."

The two young women carried the solid wooden box out of the door and into the bedroom, placing it at the foot of a double bed. Jessica noticed that here, too, the furniture was outdated but the bedding and the framed art were contemporary.

Amy straightened up. "Thanks, Jessica. Do you want a cup of

tea?"

Before waiting for a response Amy padded through to the kitchen. Jessica heard the sound of a tap running and then Amy flicked a switch. "Tea or coffee?" she shouted through.

"Tea, please!" Jessica replied, unsure whether she should follow her or not. She settled for moving back into the living room instead, taking a seat on an overstuffed armchair.

Amy reappeared with two steaming mugs, placing them both on coasters on the polished dark wood coffee table in the centre of the sofa and chairs. She then sat down too, on the sofa.

"There you go. I didn't know if you took sugar, so I've made it like mine – just milk, but I have sugar if you need it."

"Amy, I hope you don't mind me coming round." Jessica was hesitant as she started to speak. Amy's response was sure and came quickly.

"No. I've been half-expecting you, actually."

"You have?"

Jessica was surprised. This was the last thing she'd had expected Amy to say.

"Yes. I wasn't entirely honest with you the other day, and knowing what I do about people around here, I know you'll have heard contradictory stories. I thought you might turn up to get a better picture."

Jessica remained silent, hoping that Amy would continue. It worked.

"You were right the other night. At the procession. Bill did tell me off, and I hadn't actually done anything wrong so I was upset. I mean, I was a bit daft, and I probably could have worked it out, but we were on a deadline so I panicked a little. I don't really think he was reasonable. I had already checked the connection that he fixed – I am sure it was fine earlier."

Amy reached over to her mug of tea, and took a swig. Jessica asked:

"What did he say to you?"

"Oh, just what he usually says...said. That I would have to get my act together. That I would never make it as a qualified electrician if I missed little mistakes like that. Honestly, he was annoyed because I had interrupted him getting ready for the procession. He had to untie that stupid beard, bit of a palaver getting it on and off. It was nothing I hadn't heard before. He was an auld grump half the time."

Jessica nodded, and took a sip of her tea. Amy went on:

"I was on a countdown. Just a few months until I finish my apprenticeship with him, and could properly qualify and start getting contracts of my own. At least, that was meant to be the plan."

Jessica looked up. Amy's tone was disconsolate. She wondered if Margaret's assertions could have some truth to them. If she asked the right questions, here was her chance to find out.

"Why, what happened?" Sometimes, simple is best.

Amy sighed. "He was threatening to fail my final assignment. That's the worst case scenario, and I would have had to repeat my final year. That wouldnae be so bad – I enjoy the college, and more experience is always good, but..."

She broke off, and, looking around, waved her hand at the room.

"This flat used to be my granny's. I've been living in it since she went into a care home. She's quite healthy really, but she couldnae cope wi' the stairs any more and it wasn't a great idea for her to be cooking for herself. It's fine just now for me to stay here. My family actually live in Perth, but this is handy for me for my apprenticeship, and the college. I don't pay any rent at the moment, but I do pay the bills and keep the place tidy, and heated and aired out."

That explains the decor thought Jessica. Amy continued.

"Granny could go on for many years yet, and her savings are nearly gone. She'll need to sell this place to pay for her care, and I was hoping I might be able to buy it from her. I've been saving as much as I can, and I could just about manage it when I'm qualified. If I don't pass my final assignment though, that's another year on apprenticeship wages. I'll never be able to afford it on that, no matter how much I've saved. So not only will I have to move back home and commute, my granny's wee flat will pass out of the family."

Amy sighed again. Jessica experienced a twisting of emotions. Mostly empathy – as a newly independent woman herself, she knew exactly how hard it was to survive on low wages and was indebted to Reenie for putting her up. Everything just seemed to cost so much money. Saving was hard – Jessica was extremely frustrated by how long it was going to take to get enough for the slim, lightweight laptop she wanted. This was a nice, bright spacious flat, and Amy had already done a lot to make it more modern. She could do so much more if the property was hers.

The other emotion was guilt, creeping up on her. Amy had just presented her with a proper motive. She couldn't ignore it. She had followed up with Amy because she had thought there might be something to report back to the police.

And now that there was, Jessica was starting to regret her promise to assist DI Gordon and Murdo.

As the two young women continued to chat and finished their tea, Jessica was glad that she didn't have to speak to the police again straightaway. Amy's story had touched her, but her motive was even stronger than Jessica first thought. She lived alone. There was no one to vouch for where she had been after the procession began on Friday night, and it was clear to Jessica that the young woman had the ability, the opportunity and a motive to carry out the crime – so unfortunately, the police would have to be informed.

Not yet though, thank goodness. She wasn't due to meet them again for two days. As she descended the stairs outside Amy's flat, Jessica's mood was delicate. Her argument with Reenie had left her with a sick feeling in the pit of her stomach and the interview with Amy had added to her discomfort. As she stood in Dalkinchie High Street she wondered what she might do to cheer herself up.

Shopping and Eavesdropping

As Jessica turned and saw the Christmas lights and the inviting displays of the local shops, she made up her mind.

Christmas shopping. That was it. Not a big shopper normally, Jessica did have a few purchases she wanted to make for local friends. Her gifts to her family had been bought, wrapped and sent some weeks before to ensure that they arrived on time – and she had made use of delivery services, too. Nothing, however, would beat the feeling of shopping locally, just weeks before Christmas, in traditional, independently owned Scottish shops.

She started in a small gift shop. She had bought some Celtic jewelry for her mum and sisters there some weeks before, but didn't think that it would be the right choice for Ealisaid. Having observed her friend over many months, she had seen that Ealisaid favored unfussy styles – simple stud earrings, single strand necklaces – and didn't really wear bracelets or rings at all. Whatever she chose, it would have to be compatible with Ealisaid's busy lifestyle and career, which was very hands-on – no space for anything complicated or dangly.

Jessica spent some time perusing the shelves and eventually selected a pair of rose gold earrings. They weren't large at all, but not exactly delicate either – studs, but shaped like little teacups. Jessica loved the whimsy and thought that Ealisaid would, too. At the same time she picked up a scented candle for Mairead. Perhaps not very original, but they weren't very close – she just wanted the young woman to have something to open from her on Christmas morning. It was scented with green tea, which was an apt choice as Mairead didn't drink any coffee or most teas, preferring herbal blends and fruit teas.

Jessica also wanted to get something for Reenie. She had a joint gift in mind for her aunt and Grant, but wanted something specifically for Reenie to unwrap from Jessica. She had been half-looking for some time and hadn't quite found the right thing. However, now as she searched, she had a brainwave. She would buy her a Christmas decoration. This was Reenie's first Christmas in Dalkinchie and it would be lovely to mark that in some way, to start a tradition that could be continued in future Dalkinchie Christmases, whether Jessica was a part of them or not.

Jessica looked at the shelf of Christmas decorations and ornaments and found the perfect thing. A delicate little squirrel, carved from pewter and surrounded by a ring of the polished metal. It hung from a red tartan ribbon and as Jessica held it up, it caught the light. She could picture it on Reenie's tree, itself covered in a mish-mash of decorations, some of which Jessica and her siblings had made and sent over the years. It perfectly symbolized Reenie's move from the city to a different way of life in a smaller, more rural setting. Jessica, pleased with her choices, moved over to the counter to make her purchases.

This was working – she did feel cheered up. Perhaps now she could speak to Reenie this evening, and clear the air a little. Both women intended to go to the Dalkinchie Christmas Carol Concert, and it would be nice to have everything sorted out by then.

Jessica crossed the street and went into a small pet shop. She had been a regular in here since Willow had joined their family – they bought her food in bulk from here – and she didn't intend to exclude her canine friends and family from her Christmas gift-giving. The woman who ran the shop was very helpful.

"Hi, Jessica! Are you looking for more food already?"

"No, I am actually gift shopping. I want something for Willow, but also a gift for Skye as well."

"Grant Mack's lovely black lab? Oh, yes. Let's take a look."

Jessica felt that she was now getting used to life in a small village, but still the way that everyone knew everyone else's back story occasionally took her by surprise. She followed the woman around the shelves, and pondered over toys versus treats, or wondered whether she should go for a safe bet, a new ball. In the end she decided on a tough antler chew for Skye – the older dog wasn't one for toys, particularly, but was able to demolish a chew quite quickly meaning that this would be a welcome gift – and a new blanket, and a soft squeaky squirrel toy for Willow. Jessica was under no illusions that this would cure Willow's habit of trying to run after real squirrels in the park, but she was always diverted by a squeak. Plus, the toy proclaimed that it was reinforced and would be long-lasting.

Jessica decided to make her final purchase. She had gone back and forwards on this idea, but in the end had come down on the side of going for it. It neatly solved the problem of what to buy for her boss, as she had been struggling with this. Men were hard to buy for she felt; she had similar problems trying to find something for her dad, and in the end had settled on a tartan scarf. That wouldn't work for Grant though – she had seen that he had a few scarves already. Instead Jessica crossed the road to Gillespies. As the name indicated, it was owned by Gillespie MacNaughton, the local laird and Chief of Clan MacNaughton. He didn't take any part in the running of it however, hiring a team of staff to do this for him. It boasted a menu full of the finest local Scottish produce, and enjoyed a steady clientele of people looking for a treat. Jessica had only eaten there once before, to celebrate Reenie's birthday, but Reenie had so enjoyed it that Jessica intended to buy her a gift voucher for a meal so that her hard-working aunt could treat herself again.

The gift voucher would be for two, and Jessica planned to address it to both Reenie and Grant. She had thought of this a while ago, and kept changing her mind whether this was a good idea or not, so had sought Ealisaid's advice.

"Cannae go wrong." Ealisaid had advised. "It's a lovely restaurant, and they are friends, after all. I wouldnae worry, Jessica."

Jessica, however, had worried. She didn't want to come across as too pushy when it came to her aunt and Grant's relationship. Reenie could hardly fail to be aware of Jessica's feelings on the matter – they had discussed it more than once.

Jessica had never brought it up with Grant. It didn't seem appropriate – he was, after all, her boss. But over the months since Jessica had arrived in Scotland, Grant had become a fixture in both their lives, joining them for meals whenever his caring responsibilities would allow, and occasionally he and Reenie would go for a walk together – a walk that often turned into a quiet drink.

It wasn't surprising that the two of them should find the other good company. In many ways they were quite similar – Reenie had left her job in Edinburgh to start a new life in Dalkinchie, and was still affected by the early loss of her husband. Grant had moved back home to take on the care of his elderly mother, leaving behind a higher-profile journalism career. He never complained, and had never once spoke negatively about his current role as the editor of *The Drummond and Dalkinchie Herald,* but Jessica knew that deep, down, he must be affected. He and Reenie were good for each other.

* * *

She pushed the door inwards and entered Gillespies. The restaurant wasn't very big, a long narrow room with two rows of tables arranged mostly in twos and fours. For a big party, staff would happily push tables together, and it was even possible to book out the whole place for a very special occasion. Just inside the door on the left there was a high counter, bearing a sign 'Please wait to be seated.' The property had two deep bay windows, and in front of the counter there was a window seat where you could wait. On the right of the door there was the coveted window table, with an identical boxed in bench seat forming two places at a table sized for six. There was nobody sitting there at present. In fact, at first Jessica thought there was no-one in Gillespies at all. It was half-past four, long past lunch time and before the dinner bookings would have started. However, as her eyes adjusted to the light levels in the restaurant, she saw that there was someone sitting at a table near the back – a woman, facing away from the rest of the restaurant.

Gillespies had an opulent, luxurious feel. The walls were painted in a dark blue – almost navy, and the table covers were the same color but edged with a border of rich gold. The color scheme was enhanced by the chosen Christmas decorations –

small, gold sequined reindeer adorned each table, and warm white fairy lights on delicate gold-colored wire were slung across the assortment of gilt framed mirrors which served as the only wall decorations, and had the effect of opening up the relatively narrow space. As Jessica looked around, the swing door at the back of the restaurant opened and the manager came through, wearing a full-length starched white apron over a navy dress. Her silver-grey hair was cut in a chic chin-length style.

"Good afternoon, what can I do for you?"

The woman reached the counter and slotted herself in efficiently behind it, picking up an appointment diary and logging in to the computer console that also sat there – all in a couple of practiced, fluid movements.

She continued. "Were you looking to book? We are very busy over the next couple of weeks as you might imagine, although I could probably squeeze you in if you weren't too big a party."

Jessica replied.

"No, no, I am actually just looking for a gift voucher for my aunt as a Christmas present. I think you can do them? It would be for a meal for two."

"Oh yes, absolutely. A very popular gift. We have vouchers for two or three courses plus your choice of a glass of sparkling, red or white wine, or a soft drink. They do expire after a year and there are some restrictions, although not many. Which would suit you, two or three courses?"

Jessica made her decisions, then paid for the voucher. The woman slipped it inside a beautifully designed navy and gold gift card bearing the word 'Gillespies' across it, and placed it inside a thick, navy envelope which she left unsealed for Jessica to be able to add her own message.

"Lovely. I hope your aunt likes her gift, and I look forward to welcoming her and her dining companion in the future. Tell her that it would be best to book – and we tend to have a cut-off for last dining at half past eight. Any later than that, and we find people can stay on beyond our license time."

Then she nodded to the table at the back and dropped her voice.

"Not that it makes much difference. I had –" she cleared her throat, "– a party of women in on Friday night who had booked for 7pm but a couple of them were still sitting there at close to 11pm. I hope she doesn't stay as long today."

Once again she looked meaningfully at the back corner of the room.

Jessica looked again herself, and for the first time realized that there was something familiar about the woman. Surely there was no mistaking that shiny long curtain of blonde hair? And then Jessica saw the padded red coat with the fur lined hood hanging from the coat stand at the back of the restaurant. It was Samantha Johnston. Jessica had seen her here at the beginning of Yule Night, and it looked as if this was the alibi the police had mentioned.

A car pulled to a halt immediately outside, revved its powerful engine twice, and then cut out. She heard its door slamming, and then the door of Gillespie's opened and a man walked in. Neil Campbell. Nodding to Jessica, he got straight to the point of his visit.

"Good afternoon! I was told I could come and pick up a dining voucher – a donation to the Business Association Charity Auction?"

The restaurant manager nodded. "Yes, Mr Campbell. I have a note here. I'll get that made up for you."

"Thank you. I'm doing the rounds. Not many to go now." His eyes flicked sideways towards the back of the restaurant. "While I'm waiting, I'll go and see if Johnston Electricals want to participate as well."

He took himself off to the back of the room, where he greeted Samantha Johnston and sat down opposite her. Jessica noticed the restaurant manager raising her eyebrows slightly, and wondered if she was of a similar mind to Jessica – that it was a little tactless to be chasing for donations right now. Even if Samantha Johnston had been separated from her husband and might not be grieving exactly, it was still a shock. In fact, Jessica made up her mind – it was a lot tactless. Staying at the Lochside Hydro, dining at Gillespies – Bill Johnston's ex clearly was not short of money and perhaps Neil Campbell knew that. Jessica had hoped the woman was in Dalkinchie to book her flowers in with Reenie, although there might be little chance of that now that Neil Campbell had got hold of her. It was nearly closing time.

Jessica smiled at the restaurant manager, finished paying for the voucher and left.

* * *

Realizing that it was nearly time for both Ealisaid and Reenie to start closing up, Jessica decided to pop to the middle of the High Street to catch up with her friend and then make amends with Reenie, so that they could take their customary walk home through the park. She made sure that her gifts were neatly tucked down and her backpack fully zipped up.

When she arrived at the door of the café, only Mairead was visible, clearing off the empty tables. There were just two customers, both nursing mugs of hot drinks and eating one of Ealisaid's delicious cakes. Jessica realized that she had managed to skip lunch which was most unlike her. She wasn't about to order anything now, she didn't think it was fair so close to the end of the evening. Mairead would not thank her.

"Hi Mairead! Is your sister here?"

Mairead was her usual taciturn self.

"She's in the kitchen." This was the only response Jessica got, accompanied by a sideways jerk of the teenager's head in the direction of the kitchen door.

"Is it OK if I – ?"

Jessica asked before moving through into the kitchen, but Mairead either hadn't heard her or didn't care.

She went through but could immediately see that Ealisaid was definitely not in the small, efficiently organized kitchen. She must have been mid clearing–up, as it was nearly immaculate apart from the last lot of dishes which were currently in one of the large steel sinks, awaiting their turn in the dishwasher. Jessica then noticed that the door which led out to the back of the property was slightly ajar – Ealisaid must be out in the courtyard for some reason, perhaps to make use of the further storage that was located out there, or the dumpster.

Jessica eased the back door open further, intending to go out and chat to her friend. She wanted Ealisaid's take on her recent conversation with Amy Matthews, and to tell her that she had gone ahead and bought the gift voucher. However, just as she opened the door she heard raised voices.

"Craig, I don't care what you say – you cannae lie to the police! You'll get into even more trouble!"

Jessica could see through the gap. Ealisaid was swinging garbage bags into the large dumpsters. Craig was leaning against the adjacent wall, furiously smoking a cigarette.

"Ealisaid, I cannae tell them now! It will look really suspicious, they'll want to know why I never said anything at the beginning when they questioned me."

Ealisaid finished dumping the bags, and brushed off her hands, which she then placed on her hips as she scolded Craig.

"No' half as suspicious as it will look when somebody else tells them about that fight you had wi' Bill Johnston!"

Jessica stifled a gasp. Luckily neither Craig nor Ealisaid appeared to hear, either because they were too busy arguing or because the thickness of the back door blocked the sound.

Craig was replying.

"It wisnae exactly a fight. No' exactly. I never touched the man."

Ealisaid sighed, and shook her head.

"Do you think that will matter, once they hear that you nearly threw him out the pub? Honestly Craig, I'm surprised that Murdo doesnae already know. It's only a matter of time before someone connects the dots and tells them that you two were having a row. He was found in your pub, Craig. That's no' a good sign. And you found him! That makes you a potential suspect, too."

"What, you think I could have murdered him? Wi' a bar full o' people all wanting drinks on one o' the busiest nights of the year, you think I had time to nip off and kill Bill Johnston and stuff him in the cleaning cupboard for me to find later on? And why would I do that anyway?"

Ealisaid looked as it she didn't know how to answer, but then she moved closer to Craig and put one hand on his arm. He still didn't look at her, looking down, off to the side, anywhere but meeting her eyes.

"Look, it doesnae matter what I think. It matters what the police think, or if they can get a case together. I don't want them to find oot from someone else that you owed Bill Johnston money, and you'd already had words about it. That's exactly the kind of thing that they might consider to be a motive. But you didnae murder anyone, so you don't have anything to worry about. Just tell the truth, and trust the police to figure out what really happened."

Craig finished his cigarette, grinding the stub against the wall to completely extinguish it, and then put it in the bin. He still didn't look at Ealisaid, and began walking away.

"Where are you going?"

"To open up the bar. It's coming up for 5pm, time for my shift, nearly. You'll no' say anything, will you Ealisaid?"

At this he did turn to look at his friend, clearly emotional. His face looked haggard, the dark shadows under his eyes betraying his lack of sleep.

"I won't, but I really think *you* should...and I won't let it go, you know."

Craig sighed, and attempted a smile. "No. I know."

With that he left the back courtyard, using the gate rather than going through the café. Jessica quietly withdrew, letting the door close gently. She exited the kitchen, and for once was grateful for Mairead's lack of curiousity and conversation because it meant that she didn't have to explain herself.

"Bye, Mairead, see you later," she said, walking towards the main door. Mairead barely looked up, giving one half-hearted wave of her hand.

Jessica left *Lissa's,* her heart thudding. She couldn't believe what she had just heard. Craig was in debt to Bill Johnston, and had lied about it to the police? They had already had a public argument about it? That explained Ealisaid's reaction at the weekend, when Craig had claimed that he didn't have any issues with Bill Johnston. She had known he was lying.

This new understanding didn't make things any easier, however. Now she had information to report to the police about both Amy and Craig, and was beginning to wish she had listened to Reenie and stayed out of it.

Whether or not investigating was dangerous, the excitement of a mystery could also bring a heavy emotional burden.

A Night at the Church...

The Christmas lights twinkled as Dalkinchie residents made their way in ones, twos and small groups towards the Dalkinchie Parish Church for the annual Community Carol Concert. Among them were Jessica and Reenie, well wrapped up against the cold. Reenie wore a dark green felt hat, pulled over her auburn curls, and a long, thick grey wool coat. Jessica was wrapped up as she had been the night of the Yule Night procession except that she had traded her fingerless gloves for a knitted pair of Reenie's. They hadn't spoken much about the argument of the day before, and Reenie had brushed off Jessica's apologies. She knew, however, that the loan of the gloves was intended as a peace offering, and she had taken it as such. It was hard to remain annoyed on a perfect festive evening such as this.

The church bells were ringing out across the village, echoing slightly in the still, cold night. Frost crunched underfoot. The church windows glowed, the lights within illuminating the stained glass and casting a warm glow on the perimeter. A light fog gave everything a fuzzy outline. As they drew near to the building Jessica spotted Grant helping his mother, Mrs Mack, up the three wide steps into the entrance of the church. Reenie moved forward to assist further by offering Mrs Mack her other arm. Jessica hung back to give them some space. As she did so, someone put gloved hands over her eyes from behind.

"Guess who?"

It was unmistakably Ealisaid's voice and Jessica broke into giggles. She and her friend climbed the stairs.

"Where's Mairead?"

"She's abandoned me in favor of her friends. Look." A little further on, Jessica could see the teenager, laughing with a group of young people that Jessica recognized. Mairead was in her sixth and final year of High School, and Ealisaid had started to worry about what the young woman might do next. It had just been the two sisters for the past decade, with Ealisaid taking on responsibilities for Mairead's care when she was barely older than the younger girl was now. Jessica knew that this had been challenging, but she couldn't help but think that the next phase, the transition from school into whatever awaited Mairead, might prove to be a bigger challenge for her friend. She had spent so much of her time looking after Mairead, how would she cope when her younger sister no longer required looking after?

As Ealisaid and Jessica waited for the line of people ahead of them to take their seats, Jessica took the opportunity to talk quietly to her friend about the conversation she had overhead earlier. She didn't think any good would come from covering it up, especially having heard Ealisaid's views on honesty and transparency.

"I've got to tell you something."

Her friend looked at her inquiringly, dark eyebrows raised under the creamy woolen brim of her bobble hat.

"I overheard you and Craig talking outside your kitchen earlier. I'd popped in to see you and Mairead waved me through, but when I saw you were in the middle of a discussion, I left."

Jessica didn't elaborate, nor did she fully explain just how long she had spent listening, her ear to the gap in the door.

"Oh dear." Ealisaid looked contemplative for a moment. Then she seemed to come to a decision and, looking around then leaning in closer, said "no' here. I'll fill you in after."

Jessica nodded. It didn't matter now anyway. Even with the information she already had in her possession, she felt she had no choice but to tell DI Gordon and Murdo what she had learned.

They settled themselves into a pew. With wall-mounted heaters shining down on the congregation, and pipes running underneath the pews, Jessica soon began to feel quite cozy. Someone had put printed pamphlets of Christmas Carols out on the ledge for everyone to access. Above the pulpit hung a single gold star, and the fully decorated Christmas tree in the corner boasted an angel atop the highest branches. The church was old, older than most of the other buildings in Dalkinchie, and had a large organ, carved wooden pulpit and a lectern shaped like an eagle at the front.

The first few pews were lined with elementary school children and the pamphlet informed everyone that there was going to be a brief reenactment of the Nativity, as well as some songs performed by the children themselves. Jessica looked forward to the proceedings, but knowing that she would have to do a very quick write-up of the evening for the *The Herald,* resolved to take the pamphlet home and to spend the tea break in the middle noting down her thoughts in the notebook that she always carried with her.

The concert started with a perennial favorite, 'Away In A Manger'. For a moment, Jessica experienced a flashback, to the same song sung a year before in a completely different setting – Mike's little sister's school. The whole family had attended a Christmas concert there. She pulled her thoughts back to the present, where the children went on to perform a couple of songs and then their nativity immediately after that, presumably doing so while they still had enough energy. The final song before the tea break was 'Hark the Herald Angels Sing', and by this time the congregation had warmed up and were in fine voice, singing the harmonies and the melodies, with a couple of true soprano voices ringing out like bells. Jessica felt even more Christmassy all of a sudden, and was able to push the lurking thoughts of last year's celebration out of her head. What did it matter what happened last year? All that mattered was that she was here, now, in Dalkinchie where she belonged.

The hymn drew to a close, and the minister led everyone in a short prayer, before announcing that tea, coffee and a variety of goodies would be served in the hall next door. Jessica had noticed a few women making an exit immediately after the last hymn, presumably to go and set up the refreshments. Now everybody began to shuffle to their feet and make their way, slowly, through one of the doors at the back of the church that led to the low hall. It was a slow business; the church was very busy, packed full in fact, and everywhere Jessica looked she could see familiar faces. *Yes, I belong here.*

As they finally made it into the lower hall, Ealisaid went to speak to her younger sister, leaving Jessica in the queue with strict instructions to pick up a tea and possibly some shortbread, but only if Margaret Mustard's ginger shortbread was there. Being an excellent baker herself, Ealisaid was particular about her biscuits. As luck would have it, Jessica found herself in the line beside Amy.

Reenie, Grant and Mrs Mack had been served early, and had already secured a table set up in a partition of the hall.

"Hi, there." Amy's greeting was friendly. Jessica smiled warmly back as Amy continued: "Are you enjoying the carol concert?"

"Yes, very much." Jessica replied. "I have to report on it for the Herald, but I would have come anyway. I just loved all the children singing. Their little voices. Adorable."

Amy smiled. Then she dropped her voice and said to Jessica in hushed tones: "I completely forgot to ask you earlier. Did you speak to Bill Johnston's wife?"

Jessica didn't know how to reply, and she didn't really want to have this conversation in a public setting. However, looking at Amy's hopeful face, she relented.

"Yes and no. I mean, I did speak to her, briefly, although not about her husband's murder. It wasn't appropriate, not the right time. But anyway, it doesn't matter. It turns out that she was nowhere near the pub that evening, she has an alibi for the whole time. So, I don't know who killed your boss, but it can't have been his wife."

Amy's face fell. "Are you sure? She definitely had it in for him. I heard them having a huge argument in the office – more than once."

Jessica wondered what she was thinking. Did Amy really believe that Samantha Johnson was to blame for the death of her husband? Or, has she realized the danger she was in herself and desperately wanted to pin the blame on someone else? Or – and Jessica didn't like to admit this third option, even to herself – what if Amy was responsible for the murder of her boss, and was trying to set Samantha Johnston up?

The two young women had come to the front of the line and

Jessica was forced to stop her train of thought, and pay attention to the tempting array of home-baked Christmas goodies. Not just because she wanted to find some ginger shortbread for Ealisaid, but because she wanted to report effectively on the evening's proceedings. The selection of refreshments on offer were definitely a big part of that.

* * *

A number of people headed to The Ram's Heid after the concert, and on a whim, Jessica decided she would go too. Reenie headed home, not wanting to leave the puppy for too long, and Grant had to make sure his mother got home safely. Ealisaid was having a rare evening out and Jessica wanted to join her. Plus, she felt, it would be a good opportunity to see if there was anything to find out at the pub itself.

If anything, it seemed to have got darker. The earlier fog had dissipated, allowing the lights to stand out against the deep inky sky. Above them, constellations stood out sharply, and if Jessica concentrated she could see the faint blur of the Milky Way. The scent of woodsmoke drifted in the air. As they walked over the cobblestones towards the pub, Ealisaid filled her friend in on Craig's fight with Bill Johnston.

"He'll no' mind if I tell you, Jess. In fact I think he's finally coming round to the idea of telling the police."

Jessica wondered what Ealisaid was basing that on. Her own view of the situation was quite different; nothing about Craig's earlier demeanor or what he'd said had indicated he was having a change of heart. Still, she listened to what her friend had to say.

"Craig used to live wi' his mum up here, just the two of them.

They moved from Glasgow years ago, after his dad left. Craig's got his own wee place now, a flat, but his mum still has her wee hoose.

"Well, she was needing some electrical work done and they got Bill Johnston in to do it. I don't know why, as Ian Johnston is cheaper. And it turned oot that the work was more extensive than he originally thought, and he had to do quite a bit o' rewiring. Craig wisnae there when it was all decided, but his mum gave Bill the go-ahead."

Ealisaid paused, and quickly glanced at Jessica to check her friend was following. Jessica nodded, and Ealisaid resumed her tale.

"So the first Craig knew of the extra work was when a huge bill arrived. I mean, it was massive, and there was just no way that his wee mum could afford it. Craig tries to help her oot, but even as the bar manager he's no' exactly rakin' it in. So she was left wi' this big debt and no way to pay it."

Jessica was horrified. How stressful for the poor woman, and for Craig as well. She began to see where the root of the argument lay.

"That was a few months ago, and Craig managed to get Bill Johnston to agree to a payment plan. They paid as much as they could every month. It's no' like Bill to be charitable, but anyway, the agreement was made, they've been paying it up."

Jessica interrupted.

"So what was the problem now, then? If Craig and his mum were paying off what she owed, why would they fight now?"

Ealisaid looked at her. "You really did overhear quite a bit, didn't you!"

Jessica flushed and opened her mouth to reply, but Ealisaid continued:

"No, it's OK. Well, what happened wis that Craig's mum had started to get worried about Christmas, and she asked if she could reduce the payments – just for a couple of months – so she could afford to get a few treats in, and so on. And Bill Johnston said no. Craig was furious, and the next time that Bill came into the pub, he had a go at him. And he wisnae just angry that he'd said no to that, it also brought up everything that Craig really felt – that Bill Johnston had duped his mum from the start, and had done work that didnae need doing. He felt that Bill had deliberately made sure that Craig wisnae there when he told her about the extra work. So they had this fight – just a verbal one, but still – in the pub. It ended when Craig threatened to bar him from the pub, then Bill Johnston threatened to take Craig's mum to court before walking oot."

Jessica digested this. Once again, she regretted having said to the police that she would report back. The sick, dread feeling was building up again. She hadn't expected to have to tell them that one of her friends had a strong motive. Then she had a brainwave.

"But it couldn't have been Craig, could it? He was working behind the bar all night. He wouldn't have had time to murder anyone! It was busy, or so he says. And that would be easy to prove."

Ealisaid looked at her strangely.

"Well, no, I don't think he did it, Jessica."

Jessica hastened to reassure her friend.

"I don't either, obviously. But I am just thinking from the point of view of the police. A suspect needs to have the opportunity as well as the motive. So he's got a motive. But he didn't have the opportunity."

Jessica felt the feeling of dread in the pit of her stomach begin to lessen. What a relief. Now there was nothing to really report, surely?

Ealisaid was replying.

"Aye, I suppose that's true. He wouldnae have had the time."

Jessica smiled, her panicky feelings now almost completely gone. She tucked her arm through Ealisaid's as they completed the final few steps to The Ram's Heid. The old inn looked lovely on the winter evening. Without the small stage and crowds of people in the way, Jessica could really appreciate the warmth and welcome of the old building, a golden glow shining through each of its windows, the Christmas tree in open area outside acting as a beacon, and the conversation and noise that issued forth whenever anyone opened the door.

There was a rich, traditional holly wreath adorning the front door of the pub – Jessica knew that it had been one of Reenie's earliest Christmas commissions. She had done a wonderful job, the dark green foliage was still glossy and the berries a deep, ruby red. Reenie had deliberately selected the non-spiky variety of holly –"It wouldn't do for anyone to get a bit of jaggy holly in the face on their way to get a wee drink!" she had said. 'Jaggy' was the Scots word for 'spiky' and was one of the few memories that Jessica had of her grandmother when, as a small child, she had visited her in Scotland. "Watch out for the jaggy nettles!" her granny said, and Jessica, ever an obedient child, kept away from all suspicious looking greenery. She chuckled to herself. Christmas had a way of making you nostalgic.

In the next moment, unbidden, the vision of the previous Christmas came back upon her again. This time, it was a memory of Mike's mom decorating a tray of sugar cookies, some of them shaped like holly, others like golden bells. She shook her head, as if the memory would somehow physically dislodge itself.

Luckily, at that moment, Magnus Smith turned up – clearly about to head into the pub himself. He smiled at Jessica and Ealisaid. "Good evening! Are you headed in for a wee Christmas drink? Would you let it be my treat?"

Jessica wasn't sure how to respond, but Ealisaid had already answered for both of them. "Thanks Magnus, that would be very kind of you indeed! We'd be happy to accept. I'll just be staying for the one, mind, but I'll return the favor another time."

The three of them went into the pub where quite a crowd was gathered.

...And the Pub

Craig, having anticipated another busy evening after a community event, had brought in another staff member to serve behind the bar. The young woman had short, curly, red hair and wore a short black bar apron over her black pants and t-shirt. While not a uniform exactly, Craig also wore all black, although he favored a bar towel flipped over his shoulder instead of an apron. He looked up briefly as they entered and nodded his hello, then went back to pouring the drink he was in the middle of serving – a pint of Guinness it looked like, by the way he paused to let it rest halfway through. Although the pub was indeed filling up, Ealisaid, Jessica and Magnus easily found a table – one of the booths near the fire.

"What would you like Ealisaid? And you, Jessica?"

"I've got the car parked at the back of the shop. I'll just take a ginger beer'" replied Ealisaid. Jessica was coaxed into an Irish cream liqueur – a concoction she had become fond of. It was something that both her mom and Reenie had always had around at Christmas, and was made up of white wine, whisky and cream. It was quite sweet and sticky – although not as much as eggnog – and Jessica enjoyed it in moderation.

"Be right back!" Magnus headed over to the bar, to await his turn amongst the throng that had gathered there. Jessica's eyes followed him over, all thoughts of Christmas past completely gone from her head. Her thoughts drifted somewhere else entirely, a fact that was not lost on her friend.

"What are you looking at, Jess?" teased Ealisaid. It had been obvious from the minute Jessica met Magnus that she found him attractive, but, as Jessica often argued with herself, that was simply an objective fact. It didn't mean she had to act on it. It was still too soon, she had told herself – and Ealisaid – on many occasions. She had only been in one serious relationship and it didn't feel like she was completely over Mike. In fact, lately, with all the memories that kept drifting to the surface, it was almost as if she had gone backwards rather than forwards.

"Hmm?" Jessica stalled, but she knew that she couldn't put her friend off for long. The two women had grown very close in the months since Jessica's arrival, and at times Jessica felt that Ealisaid could read her mind. She wouldn't put it past her friend – it would be in keeping with her elfin, Celtic appearance. Ealisaid was slight and very fair skinned, with long jet black hair and vivid green eyes. If there was such a thing as a Scottish fairy, that's definitely what she was, in Jessica's opinion – and surely that would make her a mind-reader too.

"Yes, I was looking at Magnus. Yes, I like him and I think he's good company too, but that's as far as it goes. We are friends...and colleagues." Jessica finished lamely, realizing that she probably wasn't convincing Ealisaid at all.

"I know, you've told me this already. I just think, you know, Christmas – it's kind of magical, isn't it? Maybe you should ask him out and just see."

"Ealisaid!" Jessica was surprised at her friend.

"Too far? OK, fine. A word of caution though, Jess – don't wait too long. Life is for living. Grab your happiness while you can!"

Jessica laughed. "What's got you in the mood for romance? It couldn't have anything to do with a certain someone arriving soon, could it?"

A pink tinge appeared in Ealisaid's porcelain cheeks.

"Maybe!"

Ealisaid's girlfriend Solveig had been working for months on an archaeological dig, followed by analysis time in a laboratory in her home country of Sweden. The fully-funded project had tight deadlines, and she was only now getting a short break. Jessica was looking forward to meeting her when she came to stay with Ealisaid and Mairead for Christmas. Jessica knew that the long-distance relationship was sometimes hard for her friend, but equally she knew that both women had commitments that they were prioritizing right now. Perhaps things would change in the future.

"Here comes Magnus with the drinks. Enough talk of dating! Let's just relax and have a good evening, forget about the police, and the murder, and just focus on having some fun."

Jessica knew her friend was right, but she didn't agree straightaway. If the opportunity came up, she knew she probably wouldn't resist doing a little more sleuthing.

The next hour passed companionably and quickly, as time spent with good friends tends to do. Eventually, Ealisaid decided that she had best get home and asked Jessica if she wanted a lift, to avoid walking either through the park in the dark, or the longer route through the streets. Magnus offered to see Jessica home safely if she wanted to stay for one more, and, feeling that she still owed Magnus a drink, Jessica decided she would. She managed to ignore Ealisaid's meaningful looks as she left the bar.

"Same again for you Magnus?"

"Aye, that would be lovely."

Jessica headed to the bar to get the drinks, and as luck would have it, managed to get served at once. The pub was less busy now, with many people having headed home – it was still a school night, after all. Jessica decided she would get a soft drink this time. She had an early start herself. Tomorrow was copy deadline day, and the paper had to be ready by the end of it.

"What can I get for you, Jessica?"

She was served by Craig, and on impulse, she decided to ask him about his feud with Bill Johnston. The Carol Concert followed by two glasses of liqueur had put her in a mellow mood, and she really felt there was nothing that couldn't be worked out if they all just communicated better.

"Craig...I hope you don't mind me asking, but Ealisaid told me a little about your fight with Bill Johnston. I was just wondering –"

"Ealisaid told you what?" Craig's reaction was as swift as it was suspicious. Perhaps this had not been a great idea after all.

"Well...she didn't exactly tell me anything I didn't already know. I overheard the two of you talking about it. Anyway," Jessica continued, hoping to get her question out before he could interrupt again, "can I ask what made you go to Bill Johnston in the first place? I mean, I have heard several people say that Ian Johnston was cheaper."

Craig looked a little less annoyed than he had at first, but his response was still wary. "If I tell you, it'll go no further?"

Jessica was still trying to work out how to answer that when Craig continued anyway.

"Ian Johnston might be cheaper, that's true, but have you not also heard the rumors about his workmanship?"

Jessica shook her head.

"Well, I don't know how much truth there is to it, but I've heard that he can be slipshod, and also that he buys cheaper parts. And I've heard that the reason they are cheaper is because they are no' exactly regulation, if you ken what I mean."

Jessica did know what he meant – or she thought she did. Was Craig suggesting that Ian Johnson was using stolen goods?

"It just wisnae worth the risk, Jess, no' for my mum. At least, that's what I thought at the time. Now I wish I had avoided the Johnston brothers altogether. Nothing but trouble, the pair o' them."

Craig placed both the drinks on the bar, took payment and moved on to the next customer with a nod. Jessica didn't know what to think, and instead focused entirely on carrying the drinks back over to their table, edging past the tables and small groups of people without spilling anything. As she reached their booth, Magnus was relaxing back in his chair, his broad frame and strong arms still evident under the thick plaid flannel shirt he wore. His tousled, ruddy hair was lit from the glow of the fireplace beyond. He smiled at Jessica as she placed his drink on the table, and she felt a quick thud of her heart. Perhaps she *should* listen to Ealisaid, and take advantage of the Christmas spirit. What did she have to lose? She smiled back at him.

Magnus leaned forward, reaching for his pint. "Thanks, Jessica, *slàinte*." He clinked his glass against her coke before taking a swift draught. "I have something to ask you."

Jessica swallowed too quickly, almost choking on her drink. She coughed. "Yes?"

"Will you be in early tomorrow? I'd like your opinion on some of the photography before we lay the paper out."

He just wanted to talk about work? Jessica tried hard to keep her expression even, not to let the disappointment she felt in the pit of her stomach show on her face. "Sure, of course I'll look at your photos!" she replied, choosing in that moment to examine the droplets of condensation on the outside of her glass rather than make further eye contact with Magnus. Luckily, at that moment, a man – another farmer, Jessica guessed from his overalls and muddy rubber boots – came over and asked to 'have a word' with Magnus. Jessica nodded her assent, grateful for the interruption which would allow her to regain her composure. She sat back, taking another sip of her cold drink and glancing around from table to table as she let her thoughts drift. *It's fine just to work with Magnus* she reasoned to herself. *He's good company, and a really excellent photographer.* As she looked around the bar, her thoughts traveled unbidden back to Friday night. Busy as it was now, The Ram's Heid would have been far busier then. More crowded, harder to see what was going on. She glanced over to the bar, where the red-headed staff member was serving a couple who had just arrived in from the cold. Jessica recognized them as Reenie's neighbors. Craig was nowhere to be seen. As Jessica watched, they paid and took their drinks over to the table nearest the stove, probably in order to warm up. On an impulse, Jessica went over and started speaking to the woman behind the bar. Her name badge read 'Cat'.

"What can I get for you?"

"Oh nothing. Sorry, I won't be long. I was just wondering where Craig was?"

The woman looked about. There were no other customers at the bar at that moment, so she seemed happy to chat.

"Is he no' back? He nipped out for a cigarette. He does that when there's a lull."

Jessica nodded. Scotland had banned smoking in public places some years before.

"I'd have thought he'd be back by noo – maybe he's gone to change the barrels. Although, he did that just the other night."

"Change the barrels?"

"Aye, they're in the cellar. You have to go out, and round the building into a side door and down to change them. I hate doing it, especially in the dark like this. Craig normally does it although as I say, he just did it on Friday, so I cannae imagine they'd be needing changed again just yet."

Jessica's ears pricked up.

"On Friday?"

"Aye, later on, once the Yule Night stuff was all done and people just poured in all wanting a drink at the same time. The taps started to run dry quite quickly so Craig had to go and change them. He probably had a wee sneaky cigarette at the same time, mind. So I don't think that's where he can be now…"

As Cat spoke, Craig arrived back in the front door, stamping his feet on the mat. His arms were filled with logs.

"Oh aye, that's the other place he might have gone. To get more wood in. Mystery solved!" Cat smiled.

Jessica wasn't sure she agreed, however. For her, the plot had just thickened.

A Way of Life

Magnus' chat with the farmer turned out to be quite lengthy, and in the end Jessica accepted an offer of a run home by Reenie's neighbors. She would be home quicker this way, and so would Magnus. He, too, was offered a ride home, by the garrulous farmer. Under other circumstances Jessica would have been more disappointed, but she wanted space to reflect on the information she had just learned about Craig.

She went very early to the newspaper office the next day, and as a result ended up opening the offices. Tuesdays were busy and it could be hard to get a desk. Jessica had completed all of her assignments apart from the Carol Concert. It only needed a couple of paragraphs, but even so, as she ascended the stairs and unlocked the dark, chilly offices, she wished, again, that she was a little closer to getting a new laptop. She could have written in the comfort of her own home, she thought, mentally censoring the word '*bed*'.

So far, her plan had worked. Jessica made herself a quick coffee – she was too early to pick up her usual order from Ealisaid – and spent the next hour writing her short report on the Carol Concert, focusing on the details that she knew people loved to read about – the children, and the food.

As other people started to arrive in the office, she was glad of her early start. Grant was first, and he raised his eyebrows to find Jessica there already.

"Morning, Jessica! You're in early. Is everything OK?"

"Everything's fine. I just wanted to finish the report on the concert, and I knew that Magnus and Marian would need the desks. I think Magnus has a lot of photos to process."

Grant chuckled. "He will that, it's a bumper issue for photographs. Well, that's very good of you Jessica. Have you sent it over already…? Excellent. Would you mind starting a pot of coffee , and giving me a few minutes to review it? I'll give you a shout if there are any major changes needed."

Grant and Skye walked through into the inner office. Jessica was grateful for his arrival. Having more people in the office definitely made it seem warmer, plus Grant had a little space heater in the inner office that he tended to put out in the main one, to try and bring the whole place up by a few degrees. She logged out of her computer and did as instructed, going through to the small shared kitchen to start on the coffee.

Marian was the next to arrive. She started a mug of tea brewing in the kitchen, and then settled herself into Jessica's vacated desk. A woman of few words, she got to work straight away on the diary section, processing all the events that locals had submitted. Jessica thought that it, too, would probably be a particularly full section. At Christmas, every organization in Dalkinchie and Drummond seemed to be throwing some sort of Christmas bash. Grant and Jessica were sharing the reporting between them, and starting to feel the pressure.

Magnus arrived shortly after and immediately started to upload his photos. While his drive was processing, he joined Jessica in the kitchen.

"Morning, Magnus. Do you want some of this?"

Magnus was leaning against the door frame. As Marian came through to pick up her tea he apologized, squeezing himself back out of the way. He waited until Marian had moved back through into the office before answering Jessica.

"Aye, aye, some coffee would be lovely. Listen Jessica...I'm sorry about last night. It would have been nice to have that last drink together. Jimmy, he's a good friend of my dad's and he was wanting to ask about milking techniques and whether we were considering going automated..."

Jessica handed him a coffee, and their hands touched briefly. Magnus looked down for a second, and then up again, smiling hesitantly.

"So, did you have some time now to look over the photos like I asked?"

Of course, Jessica thought, *he wants me to do some work with him.* Oh well, it wasn't as if she had anywhere else to be. Although she wanted to spend some time putting together the pieces that she had uncovered the day before, her next move wasn't clear. Normally she would speak to Ealisaid, or Reenie, but she didn't feel that either of them was the right choice this time. Ealisaid wouldn't hear of Craig being further implicated, and although Reenie and Jessica had resolved their argument, Reenie still wasn't happy with the idea of Jessica investigating again. Grant, often a good listening ear, was too busy today. Maybe some time spent working with Magnus would help her sort out her thoughts, and work out what she could do next.

Magnus had been very busy. He scrolled past screen after screen of thumbnail images, all of them taken in just the last few days. Jessica could see why he might need some assistance in narrowing them down, but it wasn't going to be an easy job. Every image was as evocative and high-quality as the last.

Magnus had really captured the atmosphere of the community Yule Night, the magic, excitement and anticipation. There were photographs from the procession, a montage of photos inside the Village Hall, and some beautiful shots of decorative touches throughout the village. As lovely as these were, Jessica thought they might be best used for another purpose, perhaps to add to the bank of stock images. The ones people wanted to see in *The Herald* were photos of people, capturing specific events and displaying the movement of the evening. There were plenty of those as well, shots of excited children following Santa's procession down the High Street, smiling couples and families. Despite the light conditions he had been dealing with, Magnus had managed to capture plenty of detail.

Jessica pulled up a spare chair at Magnus' desk and together they categorized the images, then chose the most suitable from each category to accompany the articles in *The Herald.* Jessica enjoyed this experience, the buzz of industry, the growing feeling of competence after several months in the job. She still wasn't sure whether journalism was definitely her future path, but she felt fulfilled by the work and that she had a flair for it. Working in a small team like this suited her too, especially when that team also included a canine member. Skye accompanied Grant everywhere, and her presence in the office definitely kept everyone calm, even when working against a punishing weekly deadline.

Magnus spoke.

"Right, well, I think we have what we need here. Thanks for your help, Jessica. I'm going to grab another coffee and then get stuck into editing them. Can I get you one too?"

Jessica didn't want to hang around any longer. She was done for the day, she'd just get in the way if she stayed now, and she had skipped breakfast too. Plus, she really wanted one of Ealisaid's coffees…no disrespect to the office supplies, but it just wasn't the same. She also wanted to try and catch up with Amy again. There was something she wanted to confirm before meeting up with Murdo and DI Gordon the following day.

"No thank you, Magnus. I'll head out and let you get on with work."

Was it her imagination, or did she detect a flicker of disappointment pass over his face?

"Aye, right you are, then Jessica. I'll maybe catch up with you later. Thanks for helping me oot – you make a great photographer's assistant."

Magnus swung out of the room to the small shared kitchen. Jessica lingered for a moment, lost in thought, her gaze still focused on the computer screen. *Assistant.* As she mulled things over, her attention was drawn more to the little images displayed there. Looking at them gave her a strange sensation, and she wasn't sure why. Completely focused now on the screen, her previous thoughts forgotten, she scrutinized the display. The photos were from the beginning of the evening. Magnus had taken a few early test shots on the High Street, at the point when the crowds were gathered before the procession, with one or two close ups of families, individuals and children, and the MacNaughton giving his short talk. Jessica could see the shadowy figure of Bill Johnston talking to Amy in the background. Then the photos showed the procession get on its way, complete with Santa in the cart. He was resplendent in his bright red suit and fluffy, cotton wool-like beard completely obscuring his face. Jessica didn't know how Magnus managed to take such colorful photos in the dark, but they were incredibly vivid. She must ask him. Perhaps in her role as 'assistant.' She allowed herself a resigned sigh.

The photos gave no clue to her odd feeling. Perhaps it was just that looking at them retrospectively was sad, given the events that had followed. It was hard to see Santa waving at the children, shouldering his sack of presents, when by the end of the evening someone had taken final, decisive action against him.

* * *

Lissa's was busy when Jessica popped in for her takeaway coffee and sandwich.

"Good morning, Jessica! I expected to see you before now. Late night?" Ealisaid winked at her friend from behind the counter, where she had automatically started to prepare Jessica's drink.

"I hate to disappoint you, Ealisaid, but I went home alone. I got an offer of a ride from Reenie's neighbors and it made much more sense all round for me to take them up on it. Plus, I was actually up very early this morning. I've already been to work."

Ealisaid paused and peered at Jessica's face.

"And are you OK with that? Did you have a nice wee drink wi' Magnus anyway?"

Jessica explained what had transpired the night before, with Magnus pulled away on farm business. Ealisaid nodded sagely.

"Aye, well, you'd have to get used tae that if you and Magnus get together. Farming's no' a job, it's a whole way of life. I don't know whether Magnus or Murdo will take over the farm full-time when Dairy Smith retires, but they are both quite lucky at the moment, getting the chance to pursue other interests."

Jessica had never met the Smith brothers' farmer father, and she suddenly realized that she didn't even know what his real name was. Always called 'Dairy', he was one of a long line of Smiths that had owned and run Balnaguise. Unlike many of the other farms and crofts in the area which were managed by the MacNaughton and only leased to the farmers, Balnaguise was proudly independent. They sold their milk locally as well as supplying bigger chain stores, and it was also made into beautiful local cream, cheese and yoghurt. Jessica hadn't even considered what Dairy Smith's retirement might mean for Magnus and Murdo. They had never mentioned it, so she assumed it wasn't on the agenda quite yet. She caught herself. She hadn't even been on a date with Magnus. It was a little too soon to worry about the future.

"So that must have been a bit dull, all the milking chat! Did you just sit there?"

"I–" Jessica was about to respond, but she didn't really feel comfortable discussing this any further with Ealisaid. After she had been caught out eavesdropping on the conversation with Craig the day before, she wasn't sure how her friend would react to the news that Jessica was trying to work out the barman's movements on the night of Bill Johnston's death. As Ealisaid had already pointed out, it didn't really matter what either of them thought. If the police could build a case against Craig, then he was a suspect.

Luckily, at that moment a crowd of women arrived in the café, looking for food and drinks. Ealisaid was on her own for the moment and she was immediately occupied in serving them. Jessica had ordered her drink and food to go, and waved goodbye to her friend before leaving and heading towards Amy's apartment.

* * *

As luck would have it, Amy was at home again. This time, Jessica had gone straight to the correct buzzer, and there was no mistaking the welcome in Amy's voice. Jessica felt guilty once again – but, she reminded herself, she was following up another clue. One that might bring another suspect into the frame again, and exonerate Amy. She climbed the stairs to the landing, and once again Amy had left her door slightly ajar. The young woman was wearing her hair in a long braid again, but today she was wearing a patterned dress over thick hose – tights, Jessica knew they were called here – and on her feet, a pair of ridiculous fluffy slippers.

"Hi Jessica. I didn't expect to see you today. Are you not working at the paper?"

"I've actually done my shift already. We don't have enough desks, so when all my reports are written up for the week I tend not to be needed on deadline day. All the other staff are in. What about you?"

"I'm free at the moment. College is already closed for Christmas, and wi' everything up in the air about Bill Johnston's business, I cannae do jobs on my own because I'm not qualified, so I'm at a bit of a loose end. Although, I've got some good news – the college are sorting everything out for me. They were very understanding. They will bring in an external assessor to look at the work I've done and the reports I have been working on, and I can do some assistance work in the college to make up for the last few weeks of my apprenticeship. So obviously I have not passed yet, but this assessor should be fairer than Bill Johnston – it would be hard no' to be!"

Jessica smiled, but inside her stomach was churning again.

Didn't Amy see that this gave her more of a motive than ever? If getting Bill Johnston out of the way paved her way to full qualification, and being able to keep the flat she called home, then Jessica was sure the police would take an interest.

"Amy, can I ask you something?"

"Of course."

"Tallking to people...I've heard a couple of times that Ian Johnston was known as a bit of a–" Jessica paused. Was *crook* too strong? She tried again.

"Ah, um, there's a suggestion that his prices were perhaps too cheap and that possibly he was involved in..."

Amy came to her rescue.

"You've heard the rumors about Ian Johnston being dishonest?"

Jessica was relieved.

"Yes, exactly. Is there any truth to that?"

Amy looked reflective.

"Honestly Jessica, who knows. His quotes did usually undercut Bill's, that's true. But then some would say that Bill Johnston charged too much for labour. That's also true, given how much he got me to do, and the amount he pays me – used to pay, I mean."

Jessica waited, believing that Amy would continue. She often found that silence was better than asking more questions.

"Bill used to spread that about. He might have started the rumor – probably did, to be honest. I don't know Ian Johnston well at all, and I certainly don't know anything about tax fraud, but it's definitely something that was said around here so honestly, does it really matter whether it was true or not? If people believed it..."

She trailed off. Jessica couldn't help but agree. If people

wanted to believe something, then believe it they would, even if all the evidence pointed to the opposite. She was struck by something Amy had said, however. Tax fraud? That hadn't been mentioned. Amy wasn't finished.

"Actually, you've reminded me. Something Bill said recently. He was all full of himself, and hinted that he had proof about his brother's dealings. In fact –"

Amy screwed up her face in concentration.

"– I think he said that he had some information that would change the hotel's mind. I'm sure that was it. I was only half-listening if I'm honest, I got into the habit of shutting him out. But if that was true – if Bill had real proof than Ian was behaving illegally –"

Jessica finished the sentence for her.

"Then that would be a real motive for Ian Johnston to murder his brother."

Following Up

The next day, Jessica felt more light-hearted than she expected as she made her way to her meeting with Murdo and DI Gordon. While she had definitely found out a few things that implicated both Amy and Craig, surely this piece of information about Ian Johnston gave the police the motive that they had been looking for. Surely too, this would help to resolve the case before Christmas.

Mindful of Amy's words, she even realized that it didn't matter whether Bill Johnston had proof of his brother's misdeeds or not. If he could cast enough doubt over his work methods, then that would jeopardize Ian Johnston's Lochside Hydro contract. Having visited the hotel, Jessica was sure that the contract was worth a lot of money – definitely a motive for murder.

It was strange, the types of motives people had. DI Gordon had told her that money was the one they looked for first, followed by crimes of passion, and matters of pride and reputation. In this particular case, everyone seemed motivated by money. Craig, because he was in debt to the victim. Amy, because being failed on her apprenticeship would mean she couldn't afford to continue living in her current home. And Ian Johnston stood to lose a highly lucrative contract if his brother were able to prove his methods were illegal.

It stands to reason that he would want to silence him before he could do that. Jessica thought to herself.

"Morning, Jessica! Can I get you a wee cup o' tea?"

Murdo, friendly as ever, had managed to lay his hands on an electric kettle, some mugs, and supplies for making hot drinks. He was a favorite of Mrs Menzies, who was the caretaker of the Village Hall and ran the place with precision. No-one dared mess with her. If you found yourself on the wrong side of Mrs Menzies you might as well kiss goodbye to your social life. Everything happened in the Village Hall.

Jessica had popped into *Lissa's* on the way to the Hall, so she declined Murdo's offer. Undeterred, he made himself a cup of tea, slowly and with great deliberation.

"My wee granny always said that those who squeeze the teabag shouldnae be allowed to make the tea! 'Always leave it standing to brew', she said. 'And never put the milk in first.' Mind you, she'd no' often be caught making the tea in a mug anyway. A proper, warmed teapot, and she preferred leaves – a spoonful for each person, and one for the pot. Oh, she was a grand woman, and she made the best tea."

Jessica smiled. However, DI Gordon, who already had a drink in front of him, was barely concealing his impatience, Jessica thought. She could definitely detect it in his overly-measured breathing. Murdo was fond of rhapsodizing about tea, so it was probably something DI Gordon heard a lot.

"Is it not ready yet Murdo?," he asked. "Surely that will do. I'm keen to get talking to Jessica, here, and then get on with the rest of the day."

"Just a wee minute…that'll do it."

Murdo carried his mug over carefully, his face wearing its perpetually cheery expression. Jessica wondered how he could remain so happy when working on difficult cases, but Murdo had explained that justice and fair play was really important to him. He didn't like bad things to happen in the world, but when they did – it was important to work out who did it, and make sure justice was served. Murdo sat down with his tea, and DI Gordon began to speak.

"So, Jessica, we spoke a couple of days ago and you felt that there might be some promising leads. Once again, we are grateful for your assistance in this matter. We have had to interview everyone who was present in The Ram's Heid that evening – a very lengthy task, as you might imagine, and one that is not over yet. Remarkably, so far no-one remembers seeing anything at all."

Jessica was surprised, and before she really thought about it said, "But they must have seen Santa arrive –"

"Oh yes, everyone remembers Bill's arrival. He was wearing the suit, as you say, and was very distinctive. Apparently, however, he made his way straight to the bathroom – presumably to get changed. The pub was very warm, although the stove was being allowed to die down. It was full of people. After that, no-one remembers anything at all until the glass broke, and Craig went to clean it up. In fact, some of them don't even remember that. It was very noisy, and those further away from the bar wouldn't have heard the sound of glass breaking above the conversation and the music. It wasn't until Craig came running and shouting for help that they paid any attention. A pub full of people, all having a lovely night – and not one of them seems to have noticed Santa Claus being murdered." DI Gordon shook his head, and sighed.

"So anything you have to offer us will be very welcome, Jessica."

Jessica led with her big news first.

"I think I may have found something out that gives Ian Johnston a motive, after all."

As she explained her recent discovery, both the Detective Inspector and Murdo listened intently, DI Gordon taking notes in his small, black notebook. Murdo nodded a few times, as if to confirm what she was saying was true. She supposed he had heard the rumors in the past too.

"You say that there may have been proof that Ian Johnston was behaving illegally in some way? Using stolen goods or engaging in some kind of tax fraud? Did his apprentice…" The Detective Inspector consulted his notes, "…Amy Matthews give any indication of what that proof might be?"

"No, she didn't." Jessica felt deflated. She should have asked better questions. Maybe insisted on searching Bill Johnston's office. Pressed Amy for anything she could remember at all, anything…

"No matter." DI Gordon was talking again. "If there's something like that going on, we should be able to find it. It might take some time, but I'm sure Mr Johnston will want to cooperate fully with us, and make his affairs completely transparent. We can have them examined with a fine tooth comb. Was there anything else?"

Jessica's heart sank. She had hoped that the police would want to act immediately on this new information, and that she would therefore be let off the hook. Unfortunately it now looked as if she was going to have to share what she knew about Amy, and Craig.

She started with Amy. DI Gordon didn't give much away, taking further notes, occasionally uttering "mmm-hmms". Murdo, however, was another story.

"I cannae believe it. A wee slip o' a lassie like that. She'd never be able –"

DI Gordon interrupted.

"There's not much point speculating on that, Constable Smith. If Bill Johnston was taken by surprise, it would be entirely possible for Amy Matthews to carry out the act. He was not a very big man, and she appears quite strong to me. What really matters is the sturdiness of the weapon, and it was a very tough nylon cord on the fake beard."

Jessica moved on to Craig. Here, she was more hesitant, realizing as she spoke that his motive was clearer, and his opportunity more obvious too. After all, he had definitely been in the pub that night. And, according to Cat, had gone AWOL at just the right time too. If Murdo had any thoughts – and he did, if you went by his face which was turning all sorts of colors – he kept them to himself this time.

DI Gordon leaned forward, pencil in hand. He was as animated as Jessica had ever seen him.

"Well, now, that's very interesting. Very interesting indeed."

Jessica stayed silent. She didn't want this to be 'interesting'. She wanted DI Gordon to dismiss it as wild speculation, to come up with some reason why it couldn't be the case. She didn't want to even think of her friend Craig being the culprit, even although she knew that being the person to discover the crime often pointed to the criminal. She wished she had listened to Reenie, and stayed out of it, or could wind back time to the weekend before she had heard of this. In fact, why not wind back further to the day before Yule Night, and stop any of this happening in the first place.

But, even as she mused, she knew that she had done the best thing. Ealisaid herself had urged Craig to come clean. If he was innocent – once again, Jessica gladly remembered that Ian Johnston now had a motive as well, and had also been in the pub that night – he had nothing to worry about. They could prove it.

And if Craig was guilty? Jessica tried to stop her thoughts right there, but they continued despite her efforts.

If Craig was guilty, then he would get the punishment that he deserved.

* * *

Murdo and DI Gordon left the Village Hall, after thanking Jessica and informing her that they would be checking out Ian Johnston's motive as a matter of priority.

Jessica sat for a little longer in the warmth of the Hall, her stomach churning. The clock on the wall tick-tock-ticked the afternoon away. She came to a decision. She had felt obliged to follow through on the agreement and tell the police what she had found out. But, she reasoned to herself, the alternative also held. What was stopping her from telling Craig what they knew?

Her decisive momentum carried her all the way out of the Hall, following the High Street as it dipped down, and then climbed back up again. She didn't even pause to wave in at Reenie or check how busy Ealisaid was. The day was once again cold, and after the warmth of the Hall it had been an initial shock, slicing through her coat. Now, as she swung her arms and walked in long strides up towards The Ram's Heid, she felt her temperature return to a comfortable level.

The village seemed busier today, with more people than usual out and about – probably doing their last minute Christmas shopping, Jessica thought. She smiled and said hello to a few people, once again reminded of her part in the community here.

As she reached the cobbled area outside the pub, Jessica's speed slowed and her stride became an uncertain footstep. Now that she was here, it was hard to think of how to phrase the tale so that it didn't sound like she had gone to the police and tattled...which, she reminded herself, she basically had. She lingered by the Christmas tree for a moment, trying to calm her thoughts and think through potential solutions, while looking as if she was just admiring the decorations. Although – as she looked at it, it was clear there was a problem. As early darkness fell, it was clear to see that some of the lights weren't working, and the way they were positioned meant that a whole section of the tree was dark. Jessica moved around the whole tree, looking for other, similar sections – and as she did so, noticed a familiar figure standing by the side of the pub. Ian Johnston.

Wherever the police are looking, they are in the wrong place, she thought. There was a small fence on the left side of the pub with a gate in it. As she watched, Ian Johnston furtively tried the gate. It took a couple of tries – it was clearly cold and stiff – but he managed to pry the catch open. Then he slipped through the gap, leaving the gate ajar. He hadn't seen Jessica, who from his vantage point had been mostly behind the Christmas tree.

Jessica only considered her options for a moment before following him.

Santa's Beard

Jessica hung back briefly behind the gate before slipping through herself, once she could see that he had rounded the far corner of the building. What could he be doing? The narrow lane beside The Ram's Heid was banked on the left side by a wall, and on the right by the pub itself. Jessica walked slowly, as quietly as she could on the cold, slightly frosty concrete path. Underneath a window – that must be the ladies' restroom, she reasoned. Past a heavy wooden door painted black. That was probably the door to the cellar. It remained closed, and showed no sign of having recently been opened. Ian Johnston had walked straight past it. Jessica slowed down as she approached the corner herself. She wondered whether she had made the right decision. Would anyone hear her, if she shouted? With thick stone walls to either side and only a tiny chance that there might be anyone in the restroom at this time of day...Jessica's nerve failed her. She froze. She could hear Reenie's voice in her head.

"You might end up attacked or worse yourself."

Jessica was nearly at the corner now. She couldn't hear anything, but the cold day had deadened sound. She didn't want to turn her back in case Ian Johnston came back around the corner, and saw her retreating. She wondered whether she could safely walk backwards, carefully stepping back down the path until she reached the gate. Had there been any trip hazards? Jessica cursed herself for not paying more attention.

As she stood for a moment, paralyzed with indecision, suddenly it was too late. Without sound or warning, Ian Johnston moved back around the corner and loomed up ahead of her. He looked as surprised as she felt, his shock of gray hair standing on end – more than usual? – his eyes wide and staring.

Jessica didn't move. Didn't speak. She was aware of her mouth gaping uselessly. She sensed rather than saw Ian Johnston's right arm slowly rise, but couldn't tear her eyes away from his panicked gaze. Did he have a weapon? He probably had some heavy tools…Jessica willed her body to obey her and leap back out of the way, but for some reason – the cold, the fear – she just couldn't move. Ian Johnston's arm continued its slow, inexorable rise.

Everything seemed as if it was happening in slow motion. Jessica was convinced that if she shouted, it too would be slow, distorted and incomprehensible. Not that she could. She still thought that no-one would hear her anyway.

Ian Johnson thrust a fist towards her face. At this Jessica's reflexes did take over and she jerked backwards. Perhaps now her feet would start working too.

But he hadn't intended to hit her. Dangling from his clenched hand was something grayish-white, something that had perhaps once been fluffy but exposure to the elements meant that it was now sodden and partially frozen in chunks.

"I thought I heard something. Look!"

Jessica still wasn't sure what she was looking at, but Ian Johnson was clearly upset.

"And that's not all, come and look!"

He went back again around the corner. Against her better judgement, Jessica followed.

Ian Johnston was standing just round the corner, underneath another frosted window – which, Jessica concluded, must belong to the men's restroom. Beyond where he was standing stood an electricity generator, and as Jessica now noticed, a cable snaked from it around the corner and presumably back along the lane. It must be powering the lights. Beyond the generator were two large dumpsters, one grey and one bright blue.

Ian Johnston wasn't paying any attention to the generator. He was looking only at the pile of damp cloth lying on the ground directly underneath the window. A pile of *red* cloth. In an instant, Jessica knew exactly what it was.

Ian Johnston's voice shook as he uttered the words. "It's a Santa suit! Bill's Santa suit!"

* * *

He knelt down, and before Jessica could stop him, gathered the whole suit up in his hands. The straggly, damp beard was still clutched in his fist. He looked at Jessica with bewilderment. "How did it get here?"

Jessica didn't know what this meant, but she did know that they probably shouldn't have disturbed the pile of cloth. Well, it was too late now. She also didn't know whether Ian Johnston was simply a very good actor, but he seemed full of genuine bewilderment at the find. At least it appeared that she was no longer in any immediate danger. She took a deep breath, and replied honestly.

"I don't know, but perhaps we should tell someone."

At that moment, Craig emerged from behind the dumpsters and walked past the generator. He had an unlit cigarette in his hand.

"I thought I heard voices. What's going on out here?"

Together, Jessica and Craig managed to get a shocked Ian Johnston, still carrying the damp Santa suit, into the pub. Craig led them past the dumpsters and in through a back door, which led to a small kitchen and store room. There was a narrow table and a couple of chairs in there too. In response to Jessica's whispered warning, Craig spread a black plastic garbage bag over the table and they convinced Ian Johnston to place the Santa suit on top of it. He spoke in a stilted manner, although no-one had asked him anything.

"I was only asked to check on the – I nearly tripped over – it took me a minute to realize it wisnae…I just don't understand. What could Bill's suit be doing there? And why did someone want me to find it?"

Jessica asked Craig to discretely call Murdo. She didn't know where the police had gone, but wherever they were was clearly now the wrong place.

Ian Johnston leaned against the counter in the cramped back kitchen, and rubbed his hand over his forehead. Jessica noticed he was slightly clammy and his complexion looked gray. Craig returned and Jessica spoke brightly. It sounded forced and unnatural, even to her.

"Why don't we all go and get a seat in the bar? Maybe even a drink or something…would that be OK, Craig?"

Craig glanced at Ian Johnston and followed her lead.

"Great idea, Jessica. Let's do that. I'll bring over some teas. It's quiet just noo, it won't start filling up for a couple of hours yet. Just regulars."

Craig led them through to the main room in the pub, via the bar. Jessica had never been behind the bar before, but there was no time to focus on that at the moment. They ushered Ian Johnston over to one of the booths near the fire, although it wasn't lit yet. Jessica sat with him while Craig went to make the teas. There was only one man in at present, a wizened old chap with a flat cap pulled down low over his eyes. He sat perched on a stool at the far end of the bar, reading the newspaper and not paying any attention to anyone else. Craig must have turned a radio on, because suddenly from nowhere music began to play. It was Christmas music of course – no-one was playing anything else.

Jessica tried to engage Ian Johnston in conversation but his answers were monosyllabic. She did manage to establish that he was checking on the generator because some of the lights had gone out. That much was true, she had noticed it herself. Apart from that, he wouldn't be drawn on anything. He did seem to look a little better though, and his color was almost back to normal when Craig brought the teas over on a large tray.

"Murdo said he'd be here soon," he said in an aside to Jessica as he placed the tray on the table. Ian Johnston nodded his thanks, and picked up the tea. He drained half of it in one huge gulp, apparently unaffected by the temperature, then resumed staring into space. Craig gestured to Jessica to follow him back over to the bar. Unsure, she glanced at Ian Johnston. He still seemed slightly unaware of his surroundings. Jessica hesitantly got up, and moved over to the bar.

"What's up?" She noticed that Craig had a copy of *The Herald* – today's copy in fact. She hadn't seen one herself yet. They were finalized on Tuesdays, printed overnight and made available for sale on Wednesdays.

"Jessica, I don't get any of this at all. How could the suit be out the back? I clearly saw it on Bill when...when I found him. It disnae make any sense. But look!"

Jessica looked where Craig was pointing. He had opened the newspaper to the centre spread, where Grant had featured Friday night's events. There was the short article she had written, surrounded by the photographs she and Magnus had carefully selected the day before. Despite the current situation, Jessica felt proud. They had chosen well, and it looked good. Then she turned her attention to the photo Craig was pointing at. It was Santa on the cart.

"Well, I've had a wee look. Next door I mean –" Craig jerked his head towards the staff room, "– and that's definitely the suit. I mean the exact same suit, the belt, the padding, the fluffy beard, it's all there."

Jessica studied the photo, and nodded. It was true, this did look exactly like the suit that they had just placed on the table.

"But how did it get there? Jessica, do you think Ian Johnston planted it there? And why would he do that? Why would anyone do that?"

Craig had dropped his voice and glanced over Jessica's shoulder to where Ian Johnston still sat in the booth at the back of the bar.

"No." Jessica was decisive. "I saw him go through the gate. He wasn't carrying it then. He must at least be telling the truth about finding it there."

"OK, OK. Let's think. Why would someone else put Bill Johnston's Santa suit out the back of the pub – who would have had access to it? He had it on him when I found him! It was taken away in the ambulance..."

Jessica stared at Craig, her eyes wide. She had just had an idea. And if – it was a big if, but there was a chance – it was true, then Craig was completely in the clear.

"Craig, listen to me. Listen. What if the suit we just found was the suit that Santa wore, but it wasn't the suit you found Bill Johnston in?"

Craig stared at Jessica, confused.

"What are you saying?"

Jessica tried again.

"I'm saying could the suit – that Santa suit that's in your staff room – be the one that Santa wore on the night of the procession, but NOT the one that Bill Johnston wore on Friday night?"

Craig looked as if he was beginning to understand. He looked at the newspaper again. "You mean–"

Jessica nodded. She put her finger on the photograph.

"I'm saying what if the person that was inside *that* Santa suit was not Bill Johnston?"

Craig, stunned, looked from the photograph to Jessica and back again.

"But that would mean–"

"It would mean that we have been looking at this all wrong, Craig. Maybe Bill Johnston was killed much earlier in the evening, and someone else took his place! Can you think back? Did you notice anything?"

"I don't know Jessica. It's a few days ago, and there's been so much happened since."

"Just try. Remember, it was before the procession started. Bill Johnston would have come back in – I saw him, from outside, near the stage."

Craig squeezed his eyes shut.

"Aye. You're right. Bill comes back in and stomps off back to the gents, where he was getting changed. A few minutes later Amy comes in too, she didnae order anything – I'm no' exactly sure where she went. The pub was really empty now that I think about it, apart from a couple of regulars that won't move for anything. Everyone had gone out to see the lights being switched on."

He opened his eyes.

"How's that?"

Jessica was a little disappointed but she tried not to show it.

"Really good. You've got a great memory. You don't remember noticing anyone else coming in?"

"Not at that point. People had been in earlier, but as I say, they had mostly moved outside to see the lights."

Jessica nodded. She wasn't sure what she had hoped for – a definitive sighting of Ian Johnston, perhaps? Or an imposter, suiting up in red? If Craig had seen anything like that, surely he would have mentioned it already.

They were both distracted by Murdo's arrival.

"What's going on here then? Craig said that you'd found something – and that Ian Johnston had turned up here?"

"Yes, he's–" Jessica turned away from the bar towards the back of the room, but stopped short at what she saw.

There was no-one sitting in the back booth. Ian Johnston had gone.

Where is Amy?

Murdo responded with urgency, immediately getting on the phone to DI Gordon. Jessica whipped her head around to look at Craig.

"Craig – did you call Ian Johnston about the broken Christmas lights?"

"What?" Craig looked at her, baffled, and Jessica knew that her question seemed to come from nowhere, but she was following her own internal train of logic.

"Please, just think. Was it you who noticed that some of the Christmas tree lights had failed, and did you call Ian Johnston?"

Craig was still clearly bewildered at the question, but he answered, although more slowly than Jessica would have liked. She fought the urge to shake him.

"Well, aye, I did notice some of the lights were oot, and some others were flickering a bit, although you don't really notice in the daytime. I didnae really know what to do about it, wi' Bill Johnston being the one who installed them, but eventually I decided I would just speak to his apprentice, Amy Matthews."

Jessica felt a clutch of panic in her stomach. That was what she had been afraid of.

"Jessica, why are you asking? What does it matter about the lights noo?"

"Don't you see? Amy is not a fully qualified electrician. She wouldn't attempt to fix the lights herself. She must have contacted Ian Johnston to take a look – and you heard him. I know what he was saying was pretty jumbled up, but didn't you catch him asking who had sent him there to find the suit? He clearly thinks he's been set up to take the fall for his brother's murder."

As Jessica responded, Murdo finished his phone call and rejoined the conversation. "What's this, Jessica?" he asked.

Jessica explained their theory as best she could. Even as she went through the steps it sounded ridiculous to her ears, and it was hard to tell whether Murdo thought it had any credibility or not, but he listened gravely.

Jessica concluded: "And Ian Johnston was muttering about who sent him to find the suit. Craig says he asked Amy to look at the lights and I think she must have contacted Ian Johnston – so what if he thinks she set him up? Sent him there deliberately to find the suit, that is? I'm worried about her."

Then, Jessica had a brainwave. "Murdo! Can you go to Amy's and check on her? Make sure she is OK?"

Murdo sighed. At that moment the old man at the end of the bar, who had been apparently oblivious to everything that had gone on, waved Craig down to order another drink and Craig moved to serve him. Murdo drew Jessica away from the bar, and closer to the door.

"I understand your concern, Jessica. But this theory of yours – it's just a theory. We dinnae know why there's another Santa suit, and yours is one explanation but I'll need to speak to the Detective Inspector about it some more. For the moment, he says our priority is tracking down Ian Johnston. I'll ask Craig no' to touch the suit any more and we will take a better look later. DI Gordon is on his way here to pick me up."

A huge wave of panic washed over Jessica.

"But surely you can still go and check on Amy?"

By Murdo's hesitation, Jessica knew that she was not going to be able to relax.

"Well…no, actually. The Detective Inspector thinks that Ian Johnston has done a runner. He thinks that this is further evidence that he did murder his brother. I doubt he would hang around in Dalkinchie if that was the case. We are going to follow up a lead – the Detective Inspector thinks that he spotted his van, headed out of the village. So we won't be able to check in on Amy, I'm afraid."

Jessica's face fell as she looked at Murdo. He gave a half smile and shrugged, then went over to talk to Craig. Jessica watched their conversation play out, assuming that Murdo was giving Craig instructions about the Santa suit, but the buzzing in her ears drowned out any conversation. Murdo finished talking to Craig and left the pub, nodding sympathetically to Jessica as he passed her by.

Jessica couldn't blame Murdo. He was only doing what he was told. Yet she was still feeling very anxious about Amy. She rushed back over to the bar.

"Craig – maybe you could call Amy? You have her number, right?"

"Aye, good idea!"

He slipped his phone out of his back jeans pocket and tapped at the screen a couple of times. He put the phone on speaker mode so that Jessica could listen in. It rang – one, two, three, six times in total. Then it went to voicemail.

"I'll try again."

Craig went through the same motions again, with the same

result. He looked up from the phone and his eyes met Jessica's.

"Right. I'll go and check on her myself."

Jessica didn't know whether she was making a wise decision or not. She didn't know whether Ian Johnston had killed his brother or not. Even if he was innocent, he could definitely be unpleasant and might target Amy. If he was guilty, then he was capable of murder, and might go after the person that still had proof of his motive. All Jessica knew was that she wouldn't be able to put her mind at rest until Amy was confirmed as safe.

* * *

In her haste, Jessica leaned on the buzzer for a little too long. She found herself whispering under her breath while she waited. "Come on, come on, come on!" Her finger was close to pushing it a second time when it finally crackled to life, and Amy's voice was audible, if a little odd and distant sounding.

"Hello?"

Perhaps that was her imagination. Jessica mostly felt relief, the anxious pit in her stomach rapidly disappearing again. "Hello, Amy, it's Jessica here. Can I come up? I just wanted to check you were OK." As she said it, she realized it sounded a bit lame.

"I'm fine. Now's not really a good time."

Instantly Jessica's senses were on high alert again.

"You mean I can't come up? Are you ill? Is something wrong?"

Once again, the odd, disconnected, slightly stilted response.

"I'm not ill. It's just a bad time, that's all."

Jessica sighed. "Amy, please let me up. I just want to make sure you are OK."

Her overactive imagination was whirling into overdrive. Was

Ian Johnston up there now, making Amy answer the buzzer but not letting her speak freely? Was she safe? Even as she thought, Jessica realized there was another possibility. That Amy had, in fact, set Ian Johnston up. Hadn't Craig just said she followed Bill in on Friday evening?

"Fine. OK. I won't be able to let you in though."

As soon as Amy unlocked the door Jessica barreled through it, and took the stairs two at a time. When she reached the top landing, Amy's door was locked, unlike the two previous occasions. Jessica still wasn't reassured. She knocked sharply on the door.

"Just coming!"

After a few moments, the door opened inwards a few inches and Amy's face appeared around the side of it.

"Amy, are you OK?"

Amy's expression didn't give anything away. She looked normal enough, not ill, not scared, not as if she was being held hostage by a murderer – although what would that look like? She nodded.

"I told you, I'm fine. What was so urgent that you just had to come up?"

Jessica sighed.

"Look, can I really not come in?"

"I told you, it's not a good time." Amy didn't explain any further. Jessica tried a different tack.

"Is there…someone in there with you?"

This time Amy's response was swift and indignant.

"No! Now, come on. You insisted on coming up here, so please tell me what it was about."

Jessica didn't really have any further ideas. She went with the truth. "Well…you know they were having problems with the

Christmas lights at The Ram's Heid."

"Yes. Craig called me."

"Ian Johnston has been out and had a look at them." Jessica watched Amy's face carefully for any sign of a reaction when she mentioned Ian Johnston's name. Nothing. Not a flicker. Either Amy was a very good actress, or she genuinely didn't feel much in response to this news.

"Right. Good. I told him about the problem. I could easily have done it, but as you know I'm not fully qualified, so officially I shouldn't be doing jobs unsupervised. Did he fix them?"

"Um...I don't think so." Jessica didn't want to explain everything that had happened, but she was sure that Ian Johnston had been interrupted before he was able to do anything about the lights.

"I'm sure he'll take another look. Not sure why this was so important that you had to come up here, but thanks for letting me know, anyway. I'll see you later." Amy began to close her door, and Jessica to turn away, before she remembered something.

"Amy – wait!"

Amy sighed. 'Yes? What is it now?"

"Friday night – the night of the procession. You told me you went straight home when the procession started. But someone else said they saw you in the pub just before it."

"Well...maybe I went in and got myself a quick drink. I can't quite remember."

"Sure. So...do you think that is what you did? Got yourself a drink and then went home?"

"Yes...maybe...I'm not sure. I sometimes do that, just grab a coke and sit in one of the window seats. The pub was quiet that night, I remember that – I suppose everyone else was following the procession, and it was busier later. Anyway, I don't see what it matters. Bill was killed much later on. I wasn't there then, and I definitely didn't see anything."

Jessica looked at Amy through slightly narrowed eyes. "Right…right. Of course. I was just wondering. I'll see you later."

She turned away again, but Amy made no move to close the door this time. In fact, Jessica was sure she could feel Amy's eyes on her back until she reached the top of the stairs.

Clues from the Elves

The light from *Lissa's* window was bright and inviting in the dark of the late afternoon, making the interior vivid and clear to see. It was nearly the winter solstice, and the sun had already set. Jessica hadn't intended popping in after leaving Amy's flat, but when she saw who was sitting inside, she made up her mind.

Mairead sat with her friend Katie at one of the back tables. It was the last hour before closing, and there were not many people in the café now. Ealisaid herself wasn't visible when Jessica first entered but soon came through to check when she heard the door open. Jessica knew she had probably started winding down for the day, safely chilling and storing any remaining soup from her enormous pot, packing away sandwich ingredients, doing an inventory check. At this time of day, Ealisaid only served drinks and cakes.

Seeing it was Jessica, Ealisaid smiled and motioned that she would be out in a moment. She retreated back into the kitchen. That suited Jessica perfectly. She wanted a chance to chat to Mairead and Katie alone.

She moved to the back of the café.

"Hi Mairead, would it be OK if I joined you?"

Mairead half-shrugged. She didn't seem particularly bothered either way. Katie, however, was far more effusive, and slightly pulled out the chair to her right.

"Hi Jessica! Of course you can, no problem at all. We were just chatting about the Bill Johnston case, you know."

As she said the second half of her sentence, Katie's voice dropped and she glanced around at the other customers in the café. She needn't have worried. There was a teenage lad, sitting nursing a frothy cappuccino, working on a laptop. He wore the type of headphones that blocked out external noise, dark red cupped ones that entirely covered his ears. The only other customer, an elderly woman, sat right at the front of the café. She had a hat pulled down over her ears and wasn't paying them the slightest bit of attention.

Katie's conversational opening made it very easy for Jessica to get to the point. She wouldn't have to steer them towards the events of Friday night – they were already talking about it. Good.

"I've been thinking about it too. It's all so complicated."

Here, Mairead interrupted. This was so unusual that Jessica let her continue.

"No' that complicated. Surely the brother did it? They never liked each other."

It seemed that the locals were in agreement with the police. Jessica wondered where they had got to, whether they had successfully caught up with Ian Johnston. She nodded her agreement.

"It definitely looks that way, although it's still unclear exactly how he would have managed it."

Katie and Mairead looked at each other in surprise. It was Katie who responded again.

"Why? Surely he just got him in the pub after Bill had finished up at the grotto?"

Jessica wasn't sure how much to tell them; after all, her theory was still just that – a theory. However, there was something nagging at her about the assumption of Ian Johnston as the murderer – something not right about the way that events had played out.

"Well, actually –"

Immediately both girls were alert, eager to hear the new information.

"What?" Mairead couldn't conceal her impatience. For a moment Jessica enjoyed being able to hold the young woman's attention. Usually Mairead couldn't have been less interested in anything Jessica had to say, and wasn't shy about showing it. Now she was staring at her directly, all agog for Jessica's next words.

"There's some evidence that suggests that Bill Johnston might have been murdered before the procession. Before the grotto." Jessica didn't spell out what that meant, leaving it for Mairead and Katie to work out for themselves.

The effect on the two young women was quite different. The color drained from Katie's face and she sat, trying to process what she had just learned, her eyes flicking to one side – possibly to conceal the beginning of tears.

Mairead, on the other hand, leaned forward, eyes glittering with excitement.

"You mean that the Santa that was in the grotto – wasn't Bill Johnston at all? Someone killed him and took his place?"

Jessica wouldn't have put it quite so starkly herself, but nodded. That formed the basis of her theory.

Mairead sat back in her seat, uttering a long, drawn-out "Wow." Katie turned to her. Her voice was shaking.

"How can you be so relaxed about it? This means we were

alone with a murderer!"

Jessica hastened to reassure the young woman.

"I think you were safe. The person, whoever it was, was trying to conceal their identity. You weren't in any danger. They only had one victim in mind."

"Unless we had noticed it was a fake, and challenged him!" Katie's voice had recovered a little, and she instead sounded angry. Jessica took the opportunity to ask the questions she needed answered.

"Did you? Notice anything, I mean?"

Katie shook her head, almost instinctively Jessica thought, but Mairead, still leaning back, was looking off into the distance, a slight frown on her face.

"We would have said if we had noticed anything!" Katie was sounding a little upset again, and Jessica rushed to reassure her.

"No-one knew that it wasn't Bill Johnston in that suit until very recently. In fact, it's still only an idea. There's no way you are to blame for anything at all, and if this is correct then Bill Johnston was already dead by that point – there was nothing you or anyone else could have done to stop it. I was just wondering if you could think back and see if there was anything – anything at all – different or unusual about Santa Claus this year."

Katie shook her head again, although a little less vigorously this time. Mairead leaned forward.

"Katie, there were a few things, remember? Mind, we talked about them. Santa was definitely quieter than usual. You said it yourself. He mostly let the kids talk."

Katie nodded. "Yes! That's true! He was a lot less chatty, only said a few words – to us too. And I've remembered something else. He went off as usual afterwards, and we assumed he was going to the pub. But normally he would change before he left, so that he wouldn't have to walk back up the High Street in the big red padded suit. This time he just went, suit and all."

Jessica nodded. She now remembered Katie remarking upon this at the time. It fitted nicely with her theory. If Bill had already been murdered, and someone had taken his place, that person would have to wear the suit and the beard as a disguise – they would be unable to leave without them.

Jessica returned to her questions.

"Is there anything you can think of that might give a clue as to who was in the suit? Do you remember the voice?"

This time it was Mairead that shook her head. "I didnae really speak to him."

Well, thought Jessica, *that makes sense.* She looked again at Katie.

"Only a few words, here and there. We've been Santa's Elves for years, we know exactly what we are doing, greeting the weans and the parents, introducing them to Santa, handing over the gifts and keeping the boisterous ones quiet. I don't remember much about Santa. If anything, maybe a raspy voice, as if he had a cold? But then everyone's got colds at the moment so that's not much of a clue. There's been a few bugs going about."

"What about how Santa looked? Height, weight, anything?"

Mairead answered. "Nope, I don't think so. Looked the same as ever. The suit's so padded, it could be anyone in there. His face was covered by a huge fluffy beard, and his hair covered by the wig. Ian Johnston and Bill Johnston are about the same height though."

Jessica prepared for her final question, one she had been wanting to ask ever since leaving Amy's earlier.

"Could Santa have been a woman?"

This time, neither Mairead, nor Katie replied right away. It was clear that they were giving this real consideration, and neither was rushing to deny it. Finally, Mairead looked at Jessica.

"I think it maybe could have been, yeah. Not any woman – one that was fairly tall, and with a slightly deeper voice maybe. But actually, inside that big suit – like I said, it could have been almost anyone."

Katie nodded alongside her friend.

"OK. Thank you. Do me a favor, and don't say anything to anyone please? These are just ideas. I don't want the wrong person to be blamed."

"I still think it's Ian Johnston, though."

"You do? Why?" Jessica was interested in the response.

Katie shrugged. "Just because. They didn't like each other."

"That's definitely true." Jessica couldn't pin her finger on why she had misgivings about Ian Johnston as the culprit. Was it just his reaction to finding the suit? Or was there something else, something she had seen or heard that made her think that it was impossible? She searched her memory. Nothing.

"Thanks very much, guys. You've been so helpful. I'll leave you to it."

As Jessica left their table, Ealisaid emerged from the kitchen again and waved her friend over.

"Hey! I got a message from Craig! He said you found something that proved he had nothing to do with it!"

Ealisaid was beaming, smiling wider than Jessica had seen her do in days. She had clearly been very worried about her friend, even if she had maintained his staunch innocence to Jessica. Quickly, Jessica brought her friend up to speed on the latest developments and what that meant for Craig.

"So, as he was behind the bar all night, it really looks like he is completely off the hook! There's no way he could have put on a Santa suit and gone to the Village Hall." she finished.

Ealisaid nodded. "And do the police agree?"

"I think so. Looks like they are only interested in one man now – Ian Johnston. He was definitely in the pub at the end of the evening so he was already a suspect, especially since they found out that Bill was going to try and sabotage his latest contract. But now that he conveniently found the Santa suit – I think they must think he was actually retrieving it – and then disappeared, he has pretty much signed his own arrest warrant."

Ealisaid must have noticed something in her friend's face as she spoke, because her next question was:

"But you don't agree?"

Jessica sighed. "I don't know, Ealisaid. There's something about the whole scenario that doesn't sit right with me. Why go to such lengths? Why make it look as if Bill Johnston was murdered at one time when he was actually killed at another time? If it was Ian Johnston, why wouldn't he make sure he had an alibi for the second time, instead of hanging about in the pub waiting for the body to be discovered?"

Ealisaid looked thoughtful. "Maybe something went wrong."

"What do you mean?"

"I mean, Bill Johnston was found in the cleaner's cupboard, right? The cleaner goes in to the pub in the early morning. Maybe Ian had arranged an alibi for that time but Craig had to go and get something from the cupboard in the evening, and he miscalculated."

"Why wouldn't he avoid the pub completely?" Jessica asked.

"Maybe he thought it would look suspicious. After all, he's been there every Friday night for the last twenty years! Better to keep up his usual habits."

Jessica thought this over. That made sense. It could well be true, and Ian Johnston as the murderer was still the mostly likely explanation. Although if that was the case, it was hard to admit to herself that she had been fooled by his shock over finding the Santa suit. Her conversation with Mairead and Katie had convinced her that there still could be more than one possibility. It *could* have been a woman inside the Santa suit.

As she bid Ealisaid farewell and moved to the door of *Lissa's* she planned to cross the road and catch Reenie as she closed up for the day, so that they could walk home together to get ready for the Business Association Christmas Cheese and Wine.

As she did so she saw Samantha Johnston in her red padded coat and shiny brown boots, just closing the door of The Bloom Room as she left.

Closing In

DI Gordon drove smoothly over the winding country roads that led towards Dalkinchie. He had put his lights on when they left, the afternoon being already dark enough to warrant it. Now, however, the sun had completely set behind the hills, and he was concentrating in case there were patches of ice forming on the road. Several days of cold had frozen the landscape around them, and the Detective Inspector had the car heaters on full blast. Despite this, in the passenger seat Murdo still occasionally rubbed his hands together and blew on them to warm them up.

Their lead had proved fruitless; the driver of the van that had looked so like Ian Johnston's had taken it well, and had thanked them for their thoroughness. DI Gordon suspected he had quite enjoyed being the subject of a minor car chase. The policeman sighed. This case was ticking on, and now he had a suspected murderer at large and only a few days left before Christmas – their first Christmas as a family of four. He had so wanted to spend more time at home preparing, but the way this case was progressing, there was little chance of that.

"What now, Chief?" Murdo was, as ever, willing to take direction, and DI Gordon wished he had something more concrete to suggest. Unfortunately they were going to have to fall back on routine police checks.

"Right. Well, we shall go to Johnston's house, to his workplace, and speak to his known associates," he said. "And continually scan for his van, too. It's all we can do, under the circumstances."

Murdo nodded.

"Aye, I can definitely point oot some of his drinking buddies from the pub. And I know where he'd likely be found under the normal scheme of things. I just cannae believe he got the jump on us like that. He was right there, in The Ram's Heid!"

DI Gordon was grim. He realized that when the news had first come through about the discovery at the pub he hadn't taken it seriously enough, and now look what had happened. He should have gone with Murdo, not leaving the Special Constable to check out the situation on his own.

The more he thought about it, the more he realized that Jessica's theory made sense. Whoever had been wearing that Santa suit had strolled in the front door of The Ram's Heid, bold as brass, and gone to the men's restroom. There, he had presumably taken off the costume and thrown it out of the window and left. Or, if it had been Ian Johnston, gone back to the bar. Why would he do that?

DI Gordon stopped the car to let a farmer lead his sheep from one field into another. Ian Johnston had been in the bar. If he was the culprit, he had continued drinking at the bar. Whether or not he had intended to be there when the body was discovered was unclear – he would have to ask the young bar manager again about the broken glass that had led to the discovery. If it *had* been someone else inside the suit, then presumably they didn't stick around, although of course that would be impossible to untangle. Who would have been keeping track of comings and goings at the pub on a busy Friday evening in December? No-one, that's who.

Murdo spoke up.

"Oh...here...before I left the pub, Jessica, she was worried aboot something. Young Amy, the apprentice. That was it. Jessica had this notion that Ian Johnston would think Amy set him up, and maybe he'd gone after her."

DI Gordon frowned.

"Why on earth would he think that?"

Murdo tried to recall the details.

"It seems as if she wis the one who wis asked to check on the generator, but she called Ian Johnston instead. That's why he found the suit, round the back of The Ram's Heid.

DI Gordon breathed in through his nose. This didn't make sense to him. If Ian Johnston had dumped the suit there, then he would have been retrieving it – although why he would have left it as long as this, the Detective Inspector had no idea. If on the other hand the man was innocent, and had been framed by someone else – then he supposed it was plausible he could go after the person he thought had set him up. Did Jessica Greer suspect Amy? Someone else? Who? Not for the first time, DI Gordon admired the young woman's perspicacity. She had a way of putting things together that he found very impressive. It wouldn't be the first time that one of her hunches had turned out to be correct, and they had to go back to Dalkinchie anyway.

The last of the sheep disappeared into the field. DI Gordon flicked on the flashing lights and sirens and pressed hard on the accelerator. If there was any chance at all that Amy Matthews was involved in this case, he wanted to get there before it was too late. They would check on her first.

* * *

Reenie was in the back shop when Jessica entered The Bloom Room. Willow, who always accompanied Reenie to work, ran over to Jessica to greet her. The latter wasn't paying much attention, however, instead asking: "Was that Samantha Johnston I saw leaving the shop? What was she in for?"

Reenie shot her niece a suspicious look, but Jessica's polite, interested expression gave nothing away.

"Just some enquiries, no order as yet. She asked about pricing for funeral flowers, and some more general event flowers advice as well. I found myself pitying her, poor soul."

"Really?"

"Yes. Relationships break up, she and Bill Johnston were long separated but now she's got to deal with all this even although she doesn't live here any longer. She was quite sweet about him actually. Said how sad it was, how she would never have wanted things to end up this way even if she did want to strangle him quite often while they were married! That's quite normal of course."

Reenie gave a little laugh. Jessica didn't join in. She found the comment in poor taste, but was aware that she hadn't liked Samantha Johnston from the moment she saw her. Amy had described her as a snobby show-off, and so far Jessica hadn't seen anything about the woman that contradicted that opinion. She couldn't have killed her husband, though. DI Gordon had said she had an alibi, and Jessica had seen her with her own eyes in Gillespies during the procession. According to the restaurant manager the woman had apparently outstayed her welcome, meaning that she was there until after her husband's body was found. Jessica may have established that it could have been a woman inside the Santa suit, but it couldn't have been Samantha Johnston.

"We chatted for quite a long time actually, she was talking about returning to the area and the kinds of events she felt I could get involved in. She's very well connected and quite well-off, I could make some good contacts through her if I do end up doing some flowers, so I hope she comes back and makes an order."

"She's moving back to Dalkinchie?" Jessica wasn't sure why this was surprising. Samantha Johnston clearly still had friends in the area and probably now owned the electrician business outright. Why shouldn't she move back?

Reenie looked thoughtful. "She didn't say exactly where, just implied that she might be back in the area. She has worked as an events manager so really could put a lot of business my way. I would have to think about taking on another florist in that case. I could get a lot more done with an assistant."

Something sparked in Jessica's mind. She spoke quickly.

"Reenie, would you mind if I met you at the Cheese & Wine? I've just realized I have got some work I have to do first."

"Work? At the newspaper office?" Reenie seemed suspicious again, but was reassured when Jessica replied:

"Yes, I am going to meet with Magnus. I was assisting him with some photography. I'll see you there?"

"Of course, if you've work to do – try not to be late. I think the auction will start promptly and I want to stay only as long as I have to, then get away for an early night."

Jessica nodded. Off she went, turning right as she left The Bloom Room, waiting until she was out of sight of the windows before pulling her cellphone out to message Magnus.

* * *

There was no response at Amy's flat. *Another dead end* thought the Detective Inspector, getting back into the driver's seat and closing the car door with more force than was necessary.

"She'll be away to the Business Association Cheese and Wine." Murdo piped up from the passenger seat. "The invites have been oot for months, it's their charity event o' the year."

"Right." DI Gordon stared grimly ahead, easing the car out to rejoin Dalkinchie's idiosyncratic one-way system.

"And I did manage to speak to some o' the other contractors at the Hydro – they say that Ian Johnston turned up there earlier this evening, but that he headed away. He said he wis planning to go to the Cheese and Wine as well."

At this the Detective Inspector did turn to look at Murdo. "He what?"

"Ian Johnston's going to the Cheese and Wine. He usually does, of course, both Johnston brothers always did although at times it could be awkward – you could hardly invite one and no' the other, especially when they both ran Dalkinchie businesses."

DI Gordon paid no attention to Murdo's musings. Ian Johnston may well habitually attend the Business Association Christmas 'do', but he was not usually wanted for murder. Still, right now it was the best lead they had. If Ian Johnston was going to the Cheese and Wine, then so were they. He interrupted Murdo, who by now was reminiscing about businesses of Dalkinchie gone by.

"Constable Smith! Where is the Cheese and Wine held?"

"The Village Hall, sir!"

The Village Hall. Of course.

* * *

"Thanks for meeting me, Magnus."

"No trouble, Jessica. I wis in the village anyway, I'll be headed to the Cheese and Wine soon. So, you want to see the whole lot again?"

Jessica nodded. "Yes please."

Magnus plugged in his external hard drive, and brought up the folder of photos taken on Yule Night.

"There."

"That's every photo you took on the night of the procession?" Jessica asked.

"Every single one." Magnus confirmed.

"Can you sort them chronologically, starting from the beginning of the evening? And set it up so the photos are timestamped?" Jessica leaned in, closer to the screen. She could see that if they were sorted, it was backwards, beginning with photos taken at the Village Hall.

"Aye." Magnus performed the operations with a few deft clicks of the mouse. "Now, what are we looking for?"

"I'm not sure yet. There was just something...I will know when I see it again. I just want to get an idea of who was standing in front of The Ram's Heid before the procession started, and where they were."

"I hope you won't be disappointed. I only really started taking a lot of photies when the MacNaughton came oot."

Jessica replied absentmindedly, already focusing on scrolling through the images. "No, that should be fine..."

She flicked through the photos for a few minutes, occasionally zooming in on a particular detail. Yes, there was Bill Johnston, as he emerged from The Ram's Heid to sort out the electricals. And there was Amy, off to the side in front of one of the windows as the McNaughton took to the small platform stage to begin his speech. In the background, Bill Johnston was going back into the pub. There she was herself, she realized – her own back, observing the scene, notebook in her gloved hand.

In the next group of photos, Amy could clearly be seen heading into the pub, too. Jessica selected those images, and sent them to print as she returned to look at those from earlier in the evening. Magnus was correct, he hadn't taken many, but those he had taken had some interesting details in them. As Jessica studied them she began to see the sequence of events of the evening take place in her mind. She selected a couple of those to print, too.

Lastly she looked at the photos of the procession itself. These were more of a jumble – people on the move behind the procession, colors, lights, a bustling throng. As she scrutinized them however, she was struck by the detail. It was still possible to make individuals out. Sometimes she could recognize a person by their coat or scarf. Once again she saw herself, walking up towards the Village Hall along with the rest of the crowd. Plenty of Santa in his carriage, although she had scrutinized those earlier in the day – for a moment she looked hopefully at one photo which depicted Santa sitting up straight, sack of gifts loosely held in hand, waving to the crowd with the other hand. It had looked as if Amy was in the background of that photo, but as Jessica looked closer the likeness disappeared. Just another person with their hair in a long plait over one shoulder. She clicked print on her third selection.

Magnus had been waiting patiently up until this point – very patiently, Jessica thought, considering she really hadn't filled him in on what she was looking for. Now, however, he was clearly agitating to get going.

"Are you nearly done there Jessica? I'm needing to get away –

I'm taking more photies at the Cheese and Wine tonight, and I dinnae want to be late."

"Don't worry Magnus, these are the last ones I need." Jessica walked to the printer, and collected the photos. "Let's go."

Cheese, Wine and Confessions

The Village Hall had been transformed for the Business Association's Christmas Cheese and Wine. Lower lighting and long, draped tablecloths gave the place an air of sophistication it hadn't had for Yule Night. Easels were dotted about the hall, displaying the list of items up for auction and suggested starting prices. Two long tables held the refreshments, and the chairs were arranged in rows facing the stage. The stage curtains were closed, with a large banner reading 'Drummond and Dalkinchie Business Association' suspended in front of them. In front of the stage was a podium set up with a microphone, awaiting the auctioneer.

As she entered the room just in front of Magnus, Jessica realized she had forgotten about the dress code, and was still in the jeans and cardigan she had worn all day. Everyone else was in various stages of formal dress, including Reenie who had changed into a long skirt paired with a velvet top. Grant always wore suits, but had added a pocket square. Ealisaid looked lovely in a patterned vintage style dress with a Peter Pan collar.

Jessica recognized other faces, too, likewise dressed formally. Samantha Johnston wore an off-the-shoulder fitted black dress. Amy Matthews was wearing sequins, and had her long hair loose, flowing down her back. Malcolm McEwen looked proud and happy, wearing tartan trews and a bottle green jacket, accompanied by his wife Sarah on his arm, who complemented him in her emerald velvet cocktail dress.

At the front of the hall, near the podium, the MacNaughton stood in his full dress kilt. Next to him was Neil Campbell in full evening dress, waving a small wooden gavel around as he spoke.

Jessica glanced at herself, then at Magnus. They stuck out like sore thumbs. Oh well, no matter. Before they could greet anyone, Murdo and DI Gordon arrived, both wheezing and out of breath.

"We had…to park…miles away!" Murdo explained to his brother. Magnus smiled and gave Murdo a kindly pat on the back. DI Gordon looked frantically around the room. They all spotted Ian Johnston at the same moment, as he emerged into the hall from one of the other doors. He had not changed either, still in the same clumpy boots and tatty old coat as before. Murdo moved swiftly, cutting off Ian Johnston's exit by standing between him and the door Ian had just come through. He was followed by the Detective Inspector.

"Mr Johnston, some new information has come to light that strongly indicates that the murder of your brother Bill Johnston took place earlier on Friday evening than previously thought, and we are going to have to speak to you further about your whereabouts at the start of the procession."

The crowd gasped and went quiet. Ian Johnston began to vigorously defend himself.

"I was nowhere near the pub that early on. I didnae have anything to do with killing my brother. I grant you, we hadn't spoken in years. But why would I turn on him now?"

DI Gordon interjected.

"Because he was jeopardizing your latest contract perhaps? Losing the Lochside Hydro contract would have seriously affected your business. In fact, as far as we can see, it may even have put you out of business altogether."

"Put me out of business? I'd have liked to have seen him try – and he did, a few times, although I always saw him off. My contract wi' the Hydro was in no danger. They wernae happy that he kept interfering, but they knew Bill wis just a troublemaker. I'll tell you again, I wis nowhere near the pub at that time and I'd like to see you prove otherwise."

Jessica stepped forward.

"Actually, Mr Johnston, I can do that."

She waved the printed photos in her hand. All eyes swiveled to look at her.

"We've got timestamped photographs from Friday night, a whole sequence of them that show exactly where you were during the evening. You *were* outside the pub at the beginning of the procession. And here's the proof."

She handed over a couple of photos to the Detective Inspector who looked them over quickly, then waved them towards Ian Johnston.

"Care to explain these, Mr Johnston? This is you, on Yule Night, beside the Christmas Tree outside the pub. And in the background of this one you have actually been caught slipping in the side gate beside The Ram's Heid! Is that how you did it? Went through the back of the bar and caught your brother as he was changing into his suit?"

"No!" Ian Johnston's denial was vehement. "I did not kill my brother. I wis just at the pub to…to go in for a wee drink once the crowds died doon."

"You really expect us to believe that?" DI Gordon's tone was scoffing. "If you were just going for a drink, why sneak around the side?"

"I –" Ian Johnston didn't say anything further, he just stood grasping for the words, opening and closing his mouth like a fish.

"I know why."

Heads turned as Amy Matthews stepped forward, the sequins of her dress catching the light. She faced Ian Johnston.

"I knew I had checked those connections! You sabotaged the electrics, didn't you? Made the sound system fail?"

Ian Johnston didn't say anything. Then he looked downwards, and said something very softly.

"What was that?" Amy's voice rang out clearly, full of indignation.

"I said, aye. Aye, I did loosen the connections."

He looked up again, regaining energy as he spoke.

"Well, you can hardly blame me, can you? Bill wis always trying to ruin my business! Spreading false rumors aboot stolen goods…tax fraud…calling up the contracts and making life hard for me. Just this one time I thought I'd have a wee joke at his expense."

"At my expense, you mean!" Amy had turned pink, and her eyes glittered in anger. "I got the blame!"

The Detective Inspector stepped forward, clearing his throat.

"Excuse me, could we return to the matter in hand? What did you do, Mr Johnston, after you loosened the connections?"

"I just stayed behind the gate until the coast wis clear and the crowd moved away, then I went into the pub."

"A likely story –" began the Detective Inspector, but Jessica interrupted him.

"Actually, I think that's true. Look, I've got another photo."

She handed another photograph to DI Gordon. He looked at this one then passed it back to Jessica in frustration.

"I don't know what I'm looking at. Can you explain?"

"Look!" Jessica pointed to the photo. "You can't see his face, but that is Ian Johnston, I'm almost sure of it. It's his arm, the arm of his coat. The mended patch there, it's exactly like his."

The Detective Inspector looked up at Ian Johnston who obligingly stuck out his left arm. Murdo, beside him, called out:

"I can confirm, Sir, that there is a worn patch here on the arm of this coat. It looks like it has been pattern darned with a blue thread…no, here, I've made a mistake. That's just a simple running stitch."

The Detective Inspector looked at the photo, then up at Ian Johnston, then at the photo again and finally at Jessica.

"But this photo – it was taken –"

"After the float with Santa had already left, yes. With the imposter Santa on board."

"So that means that it couldn't have been Ian Johnston." DI Gordon looked to Jessica for confirmation

"I already telt ye that!" There was no relief evident in Ian Johnston's voice, only the usual grumpiness.

DI Gordon spoke directly to Jessica.

"You eliminated Ian Johnston. Who else? Did anyone else turn up in those photos of yours?"

"No. I thought I saw Amy in one of them, but I was mistaken."

"Ah yes, Amy Matthews. What was it you said about her? That she may have set Ian Johnston up?"

"You said what?" Amy had barely calmed down from her interaction with Ian Johnston, and now she directed her fury at Jessica.

The latter tried to placate her. "No, Amy, I said I thought that

Ian Johnston might think you had set him up – I honestly didn't know what to think. You must admit, it doesn't look good for you. I wasn't sure for a while. But I am pretty sure now. You had a lot to gain from Bill Johnston's death, and a lot to lose if things continued the way they was going. You argued with him on Yule Night, and followed him in to The Ram's Heid just before he was murdered. We only have your word that you went for a drink and then went home. I spoke to some witnesses that believed that Santa could have been impersonated by a woman. And you did seem very keen to point the finger at someone else."

Amy stood very straight. When she spoke, her voice was small, but not shaky.

"I didn't do it. I've got no proof, I went home on my own and didn't see any of my neighbors, but I didn't do it."

"It's all right, Amy, I know you didn't." Jessica smiled at the young woman.

DI Gordon's head whipped to Jessica. "You do?" Jessica ignored him, instead directing her next remark straight at Ian Johnston.

"There's something I am not clear about. I can prove that you were not the person who strangled your brother, but why did you run off from the pub this afternoon? I think I know, but I just wanted to be sure."

Ian Johnston looked at her. "For the same reason that I'm here now."

The Detective Inspector looked nonplussed, but Jessica nodded. "You went to find her, didn't you." It was a statement, rather than a question. Ian Johnston's eyes met hers, and he replied.

"I went to the Hydro and she wisnae there – this was the next place to check."

DI Gordon looked from one to another again. "Who? Who are you talking about?"

Ian Johnston wheeled around and pointed, exclaiming: "Her!" at the exact same moment as Jessica said, "Samantha Johnston!"

"Me?"

Samantha Johnston's hand flew to her chest. "Ian, I am not sure how you think I can help – I am very sorry about what happened to Bill, but –"

Ian Johnston's voice was low and treacherous. "It was you that killed him, it must have been. There was no love lost between me and Bill, but you, you really hated him. I know you did. I don't know how you pulled it off, but you must have done it somehow. And made it look like it was me!"

DI Gordon interjected. "Mrs Johnston has an alibi for Friday evening."

Samantha Johnston continued. "That's right! I was in Gillespies all evening long, so I am not sure how you think I managed to murder my ex-husband. At the time he died I was enjoying my lemon cheesecake – and very nice it was too!" She had faintly emphasized the word *ex*.

Jessica spoke up. "Well, he wasn't actually murdered during your dessert, Mrs Johnston. No, he was killed much earlier – probably just as you ordered."

For the first time Samantha Johnston looked a little uncertain. "What – what do you mean? Bill did Santa's grotto that night, just like he always did. He was murdered in the pub after that."

At this, the Detective Inspector placed a hand on Jessica's arm as if to suggest she not say any more, but Jessica wouldn't be stopped.

"No. That was an imposter. Someone murdered Bill as the

Christmas lights were turned on, took Bill's place on the float wearing a Santa suit, and handed out gifts in the grotto. Then that someone walked up the hill to The Ram's Heid, made sure they were seen arriving, went to the rest room and threw the extra Santa suit out of the window – where we found it earlier today. This someone not only knew Bill's habit of going to The Ram's Heid after the grotto, but knew that Ian Johnston would be there too – a useful scapegoat."

Jessica paused. She took a deep breath.

"Unfortunately – for you, that is – they left a bit of a trail." She passed another photo to DI Gordon, and pointed out a detail on it. He raised one eyebrow.

"You see, Mrs Johnston, they knew all that because you told them. You did plot to murder your husband, although you didn't carry it out yourself. You got someone else to do it for you."

Samantha Johnston seemed lost for words. When she eventually found her voice, she replied: "Oh…really? And exactly how, I mean who…" She cut herself off, and drew herself up straighter. "You don't have any evidence."

"I've got this time-stamped photo of a car, parked beside the pub when the owner claimed to be at home, laid up with a bad cold." She handed over the photo to DI Gordon, this time ensuring she pointed out the time stamp, and the distinctive number plate on the gunmetal Range Rover. NE17 CAM.

"Plus, we have the Santa suit." She looked to DI Gordon for confirmation. He nodded.

"It has been exposed to the elements for a few days, but I'm confident we'll get some DNA from it. It's probably best if you both cooperate with the investigation from now on."

His tone was chilly. His expression meant business. He

looked squarely at Samantha Johnston. Her face began to contort, rapidly turning a dark red. She turned her head, and started to shout at Neil Campbell.

"You idiot! I told you to move the suit!"

"You told me…? That's ridiculous. You were meant to move it, not me! How on earth did you expect me to go creeping around the pub again? I'm sure you said that you'd go back for it."

"No! I made it perfectly clear! It was your job!"

"Oh yes, and what was your job again? Sitting with your friends, and enjoying an expensive meal, that's right. While I did all your dirty work!"

"My dirty work? You wanted him dead just as much as I did! Let's get married, you said. We will be a power couple, you said. Just the small inconvenience of my husband standing in our way! This is all your fault – and I didn't lay a hand on anyone. It won't be me that goes down for it."

"Why, you –"

The next events happened in a blur. Neil Campbell made a run for Samatha Johnston, raising his gavel-holding hand as he went. Then the MacNaughton intervened, easily bringing Neil Campbell to the ground with a well-timed tackle. One knee held Neil Campbell flat on his front as the MacNaughton grabbed his wrist, and forced him to relinquish the wooden gavel. It was all over in seconds.

"Is that what you'd call a citizen's arrest?" Murdo asked. He was still standing beside Ian Johnston, who looked sickened again, much as he had earlier.

"No, Constable Smith." The Detective Inspector replied. "This would just be a standard arrest."

Christmas Eve

Ealisaid walked around the large table, placing dishes of cranberry sauce and something that she called bread sauce at strategic intervals. She had pushed several of her tables together to make one long dining space.

Jessica, who had been helping with the preparations all afternoon, stood back and surveyed the result. It looked spectacular. You wouldn't have been able to tell that there were several café tables under there – it looked seamless. Ealisaid had produced an enormous, heavy sea-green tablecloth which blanketed the tables and draped beautifully to the ground. Her accessories were of a red tartan – tartan napkins, tartan place mats and tartan ribbon wound around the sprigs of mistletoe she had dotted around on the table. In the centre, two creamy church candles sat on antique gold holders.

This Christmas Eve dinner had been a plan of Ealisaid's all along, and she had ramped it up after the events of the Business Association evening. Instead of doing a full Christmas dinner, she had instead opted for a themed buffet, with platters of cold roast turkey and baked ham sitting on the counter, potato salad, fresh bread, a carrot dish that contained slivered almonds, and red pickled cabbage. The sauces would complement the meats, and Ealisaid had also added a grainy Scottish mustard for those who liked it. To follow, there were oatcakes, cheeses, grapes and Christmas cake.

It was a beautiful spread. And Jessica was looking forward to enjoying it with friends. Finally, her dream of a perfect Scottish Christmas was being realized. And they still had the big day itself to come.

Reenie arrived first, along with Grant.

"Oh Ealisaid, this looks amazing! Thank you so much. It's lovely not to have to think about cooking on Christmas Eve."

Jessica was on drinks duty, and poured a glass of prosecco for Reenie and sparkling elderflower for Grant, who was driving. No sooner had she handed them over than Craig arrived, bashfully ushering in Cat in front of him. Her short red hair was clipped back with a barrette, and she wore a lot of sparkly make-up which enhanced her blue eyes.

"We'll both need to be up at the pub by nine o'clock," Craig said anxiously, but Ealisaid soon reassured him.

"Eat as much or as little as you like, and leave whenever you need to. No formalities here!"

Craig nodded his thanks as he and Cat removed their layers of outerwear, and hung them over the backs of chairs.

Next to arrive were Murdo, Magnus and DI Gordon. The Smith brothers both wore kilts and thick knitted Christmas sweaters, and Jessica worried for the state of their knees. Surely their legs must be frozen? They didn't seem to feel it however, sweeping in with broad smiles. Magnus' sweater showed a Christmas tree, patterned with brightly colored knitted tinsel wrapped around the tree. Murdo's bore an illustration of Rudolph the reindeer, complete with a suitably incredible shiny red nose. It appeared to be shot through with some sparkly yarn. Jessica wondered if Murdo had knitted these, too.

Ealisaid greeted the trio. "I'm glad you could make it, Detective Inspector!"

"I'm not staying for food," replied DI Gordon with a nod towards her. "I want to go and spend the evening with my family, and if I leave now I will be back in time for bath-time. We've got some new traditions to make. However, I thought I would pop in and have a quick drink, and thank you all. After all, without your help I wouldn't be able to spend much time with my family this Christmas at all."

He too accepted a glass of sparking elderflower, and raised it to the assembled group. Everyone raised their drinks in response, and as they did so, Ealisaid called out:

"Oh Reenie! Look! Look where you are standing!"

Ealisaid glanced at Jessica and gave her a wink. Jessica looked over. Reenie and Grant had found themselves underneath some strategically hung mistletoe. Both laughed, and leaned in for a kiss. Eyes wide, Jessica watched as they broke apart and as they did so, she saw Magnus standing behind them, looking at her. The eye contact lasted for several seconds and Jessica felt her stomach flip as Magnus smiled slowly.

The door opened and Amy arrived, bearing bottles of ginger wine for Ealisaid and Jessica, and full of apologies for her strange behavior when Jessica had visited. "I was in the middle of making this for you, and I didn't want you to see! You must have thought me so rude." Jessica and Ealisaid accepted the gifts gratefully. After hearing Amy's story, they had both resolved to try and get to know the soon-to-be qualified electrician better. Jessica, because she knew what it was like to end up living in Dalkinchie – and at least she had family in the village. Amy's family wasn't far away, it was true, but she was making her own life in a new place, and this resonated with Jessica. Ealisaid had an ulterior motive.

"I'd far rather deal wi' Amy than Ian Johnston, when I've got anything needing sorted at home or in *Lissa's.* Honestly, you wouldn't believe how I've been spoken to over the years – as if I know nothing, and I'm just an ignorant wee lassie playing at running a business. Well, a decade later and I'm doing OK, thank you very much, but I'd still rather talk to somebody who gives me the right information and doesnae act like my questions are stupid. Plus, I'd love to support another young woman in business in Dalkinchie."

Now Ealisaid smiled and introduced Amy to Reenie. Jessica, pouring Amy's drink, was sure that Reenie would feel similarly about working with Amy. There was definitely some work needing done in The Bloom Room cellar.

Last, but by no means least, in came Mairead, accompanied by Solveig, Ealisaid's girlfriend. The latter had arrived the day before, but had been happy with Ealisaid's plan to spend the day cooking because she had saved up her Christmas shopping until the last minute. She had therefore taken Mairead to Perth for the day – "Rather her than me," Ealisaid had remarked – and the two of them burst through the door laughing. Jessica had never seen Mairead so relaxed and cheerful. She was clearly very fond of Solveig.

This was the first time Jessica and Solveig had met. She saw a petite woman, with blond hair tied back in a practical pony tail. She was wearing a thick, fair isle sweater, cream and patterned with navy, green and red. Her cheeks were rosy from the cold outside, and her eyes glittered.

"It's yourself, Solveig!"

Murdo was immediately by her side, wrapping her in a huge bear hug. When Solveig spoke, it was in perfect, if slightly accented English.

"Murdo, I am so very pleased to see you again. How are you?"

"Oh, I've lots of news to fill you in on. Sit by me, and we'll catch up."

Solveig laughed. "I have a lot of catching up to do!"

Magnus chimed in. "You do that! Tell, me, where exactly have you been? I'd love to visit some of your dig locations some day, and take photos."

"I would love that too, Magnus."

Clearly Solveig was already well known in Dalkinchie. Jessica caught Ealisaid's eye, and the latter moved to Solveig and drew her over.

"Before you get settled in, there's some new people I would like you to meet."

Reenie and Grant were standing nearby, and Grant raised his glass. "Merry Christmas, Solveig. Lovely to see you again."

"Merry Christmas, Grant!"

Ealisaid introduced Reenie and Jessica.

"Solveig, this is Reenie. Remember I told you she moved to the village in the summer and set up a new flower shop across the road? Solveig nodded. "Yes, of course. Nice to meet you, Reenie."

Ealisaid continued.

"Reenie, my girlfriend Solveig. She spends most of her time in exotic locations up to her arms in mud. We met here when she was on a dig location nearby."

Reenie switched her glass to her other hand in order to shake Solveig's.

"And you. It must be nice to be back in Dalkinchie for Christmas."

"It is, thank you. I always like coming here. It is so...peaceful."

Reenie's only response was a small smile, but her eyes met Jessica's. Ealisaid now turned to her friend.

"And this is Jessica, Reenie's niece."

Solveig turned to Jessica and smiled warmly. "Jessica, I have heard so much about you. It is nice to finally meet. You are also not from Scotland, I believe? Tell me, how do you find it?"

Jessica smiled back.

"It is lovely to meet you, too. And yes, as you can probably tell, I'm American, although my mom is Scottish. I've been here six months now. And how do I find it? Well…"

Jessica paused. It was hard to put into words exactly how she felt about Scotland now. Her initial holiday had turned into an extended stay, and she was surrounded by family, friends and work she found fulfilling. She had felt 'unfinished' when she graduated, feeling that she had to push on to the next phase, the next qualification, the next stage of life. Here, she felt free of that, able to focus on everyday details in a way she hadn't managed for a while, let life unfold as it may.

This confusion of thoughts all went through her mind simultaneously. She looked at Solveig again, who was still waiting expectantly for her reply. Jessica continued her answer.

"Home. Scotland feels like home to me now."

Author's Note

Like Jessica, I love Christmas and I always wanted to set one of the Dalkinchie books at that time of year. Cozy Christmas mysteries are amongst my favourites to read, so I suppose it stands to reason that I wanted to write one!

Christmas in Scotland is a mish-mash of different traditions. Much of it stems from the Victorians, with their Christmas trees, cards and crackers – all of which are very popular still today. We eat a roast turkey dinner with all 'the trimmings' – sausages wrapped in bacon ('pigs in blankets'), cranberry sauce, roast and mash potatoes, Brussel sprouts, red cabbage carrots, stuffing and plentiful gravy. There are, of course, many variations on that theme, and most families these days will find themselves catering for vegetarian and vegan diets as well, my own included. We set the Christmas pudding ablaze by dousing it with rum, but usually have a chocolate dessert option as well.

None of this, however, is particularly Scottish, which is part of the reason that I didn't include the Christmas Day scene in this book. (The other was that I wanted the celebratory aspect of all the characters coming together at the end, which made more sense on Christmas Eve). Scotland, historically, had a low-key Christmas. Christmas Day did not become a public holiday until 1871 and the day after, Boxing Day, in 1974. We saved our main celebration for New Year's Eve – Hogmanay, where there are plentiful Scottish traditions. I will definitely feature these in a future book.

The Lochside Hydro is fictional, but there are a scattering of Hydro hotels across Scotland with the same history and origins that I described. They are all very luxurious, and well worth a visit.

Thank you for joining me in Dalkinchie once again, and I look forward to welcoming you to a Clan Gathering at Castle Drummond for the next tale in the series, *Death in the Clan!* If you want to stay in touch with me along the way, and learn more about the process of writing the Dalkinchie mysteries, then read on to find out how to join my mailing list. (There's a free bonus story for you, if you do…)

With all best wishes,

Carly R.

Join my mailing list

Dinner at Gillespies

CARLY REID

I have written a bonus, extra scene for readers of *Mince Pies and Murder.* If you want to know what happens when Reenie and Grant use their gift voucher from Jessica, and dine out together in Gillespies restaurant then please visit this link: https://BookHip.com/CGVNJP.

In exchange for this story, you will be asked to sign up to my mailing list – just follow the instructions on the BookFunnel page. I send out my newsletter approximately every three weeks, with the latest news on my writing and my life. I share promotions, sales and launches of new books from other cozy authors. I also always include my Scots Dictionary Corner which introduces and explains some of the vocabulary my characters use.

If you are already subscribed to my mailing list then please don't worry – this story will be sent out as an extra every December. If you are reading this at any other time of year, and just can't wait that long, please feel free to email me directly at info@carlyreid.com. Put 'Gillespies' in the subject line, and I'll send you the link.

Enjoy *Dinner at Gillespies!*

About the Author

Carly Reid is the author of the Dalkinchie Mystery series. She is an avid reader who has loved books and stories since childhood, her favourites being cozy mysteries and Golden Age crime. After a career working in all aspects of the book trade, Carly decided it was time to write her own stories. The Dalkinchie Mystery series is the result.

Carly lives in Scotland with her family, although not in Dalkinchie!

You can connect with me on:

http://www.carlyreid.com

http://fb.me/CarlyReidAuthor

Subscribe to my newsletter:

https://bookhip.com/CGVNJP

Also by Carly Reid

The Dalkinchie Mysteries are a series of contemporary cozy mysteries set in Perthshire, Scotland. The reading order is:

Murder in Bloom (a novella)

Death in Dalkinchie

Mince Pies and Murder

Dinner at Gillespies (an exclusive short story for mailing list subscribers)

Death in the Clan

Murder in Bloom

A Dalkinchie Mysteries Novella

A bad breakup, a new business...

...and a body in the cellar.

When Jessica Greer comes to Scotland to help Aunt Reenie set up a new flower shop, she plans to get over her ex-boyfriend and find some comfort in her ancestral home – as well as help Reenie get ready for opening day. But when the local estate agent turns up dead in the new shop cellar, and the locals seem keen to pin the crime on an outsider, Jessica finds herself drawn in to the events, secrets and drama of a not-so-sleepy Scottish village.

Death in Dalkinchie

Dalkinchie Mysteries Book 1

It's the annual Dalkinchie Craft Show, and one thing seems certain – Margaret Mustard's orange and whisky marmalade will take top prize, again.

Jessica Greer is settling in to life in a Scottish village, balancing her job as a junior reporter with new friendships and attempting to house-train Willow, her Aunt Reenie's spaniel puppy. When the head judge is poisoned as Jessica reports on the Craft Show, her extensive notes, observational skills and ability to be in the wrong place at the right time are put to the test again. Can Jessica narrow down the list of suspects to find the killer before there's another victim?

If you love locked room mysteries, quirky characters, and a Scottish small-town setting, you'll love *Death in Dalkinchie.*

Made in the USA
Columbia, SC
06 December 2024

48476276R00102